The Strange
but Wonderful
Cosmic Awareness
of Duffy Moon

The Strange but Wonderful Cosmic Awareness of Duffy Moon

by Jean Robinson

drawings by Lawrence Di Fiori

 Houghton Mifflin/Clarion Books/New York

Third Printing
Houghton Mifflin/Clarion Books
52 Vanderbilt Avenue, New York, NY 10017

Text copyright © 1974 by Jean Robinson
Illustrations copyright © 1974 by Houghton Mifflin/Clarion Books
Designed by Paula Wiener
Printed in the United States of America

Library of Congress Cataloging in Publication Data
Robinson, Jean
The strange but wonderful comic awareness of Duffy Moon.

Summary: Picked on by younger boys, Duffy Moon becomes a student of Cosmic
Awareness and develops talents and powers beyond those he expected.
[1. Humorous stories] I. Di Fiori, Lawrence, illus. II. Title.
PZ7.R5663St   [Fic]   73-15526   ISBN 0-395-28880-0

(Previously published by The Seabury Press under ISBN 0-8164-3115-9)

To those who dream of being what they can't,
and those who work at being what they can.

The Strange
but Wonderful
Cosmic Awareness
of Duffy Moon

Chapter 1

I'D NEVER tell my friend Duffy this, but I feel sure that somewhere in the world, Dr. Flamel still thinks of him as one of his best students. Maybe he's even using him in an ad, as Case #546 or something, though if people ever knew the truth—what cosmic awareness actually did to Duffy Moon—they'd think twice about signing up themselves.

It was getting beat up so much that got Duffy interested in cosmic awareness, I guess. That, and the fact that he was really small for an eleven year old and touchy about it besides. I didn't see where it made that much difference, because even at parades, a kid can go early and sit on the curb. But, for Duffy—who was not only small, but had a baby face, too—every day was just full of reminders that he was a peanut. We'd go to the library and the lady would ask him if he wanted to come for story hour. We'd get in place for a class picture and Duffy would be stuck up front with the girls on a little stool.

But being teased so much about his size, that was the worst thing. It was what got him into so many fights, if you want to know the truth. Let somebody call Duffy "shrimp" and right away he'd sputter and turn red. Then before you knew it, there'd be more words and up would go Duffy's fists, no matter how big the other kid was.

He had spirit, but it was never enough. If somebody wasn't there to stop the fight, the other kid would clobber him and Duffy would wind up even touchier than before. It was a vicious circle, and not one that was likely to end as far as I could see.

And I knew Duffy better than anyone, on account of us being best friends and living on the same block. We were kind of by ourselves there, if you know what I mean. All the other kids were either babies or eighth- and ninth-graders who didn't want anything to do with us. Some were even older, but then it *was* an old neighborhood and most of the adults were grandparents with their kids grown up and gone.

The reason I mention this is so you'll understand how Duffy and I got to be buddies. What isn't easy to understand is why I was so slow to suspect trouble that afternoon last June when this whole thing began.

It was well after four o'clock. Channel 4 had already started its afternoon horror film, I had the Monopoly board all set up for our regular after-school game and Duffy—who had promised to come in time for the movie—was nowhere in sight.

"So where are you?" I snapped into the phone. "You've already missed the first part where they explain the whole story. You know how hard it is to catch up after that!"

Duffy's voice is scratchy and kind of deep for his age, but that afternoon it was at least an octave higher.

"I c-can't explain now," he croaked and I could almost see him looking over his shoulder. "Can you c-come down here? It's a matter of life or death, Peter. I've got to have your help!"

I was used to Duffy acting dramatic—it went along with him being excitable and all—but this time he really sounded serious. So I put aside my plans, including the one to play ball with my Yorkshire Terrier, Dodger, and told Duffy I'd be right over.

"Listen for the bell, will you? I should be there in about five minutes."

Unlike my dad and me, who live in this Victorian monstrosity we had before my mother died, Duffy lives with his aunt and uncle in the apartment building on the corner. It's not a bad place, if you like apartments, and Duffy has a room of his own, a half bath and one of those eight-inch TV's.

The TV is so he can watch his Uncle Ralph Randall, who is Captain Smiles on an afternoon kiddie show. For most kids, living with a TV star like Captain Smiles would be great. For Duffy, it is just kind of confusing. I mean, as big and jolly as his Uncle Ralph is with kids on the tube, off-screen he doesn't want that much to do with them.

Duffy's Aunt Peggy—who is short like him—is just the opposite.

"Peter Finley! I'm so *glad* you're here," she said when she all but pulled me into their apartment that afternoon. "Maybe you can find out what happened. I couldn't. One minute, Duffy and Niagara Joe are on their way to your house and the next thing I know, they're back home and Duffy's shut up in his room!"

I should explain about Niagara Joe, who actually has a pretty important part in this story. He is Duffy's blue budgie, a really kooky bird that takes the place of a dog for him and goes almost everyplace he does. In fact, Duffy even bought him a special cage just for that purpose—a

Tiny Traveler, it's called—and Niagara Joe rides around in it like he's King Tut.

Wondering if maybe something had happened to Joe on the way over to my house, I trudged down the hall to Duffy's bedroom. The hand lettered sign on the door read "No Admittance Except on Invitation," but I had what I guessed was a bona fide invitation, so I knocked and waited for an answer. Aunt Peggy waited, too, but a little way down the hall where she figured she wouldn't be noticed.

"It's Peter, Duffy. Okay if I come in?"

There was a long period of silence. Then the lock on the knob clicked and the door opened just a crack.

"What's going on?" I asked when Duffy let me inside. He had his face turned away from me so I was more or less talking to Niagara Joe, who was perched on his left shoulder.

"Duffy, look at me! You scared of something? What happened?"

Slowly, Duffy faced me square and I could tell right away why he'd sneaked into the apartment past his Aunt Peggy. He had another shiner—a really spectacular one this time. Worse even than the black eye he'd gotten two summers before when he tangled with the Bonner twins over his place in the lunch line.

"Gee," I marveled, resisting the impulse to touch it. "Who gave it to you?"

Duffy shook his head. Then he picked up a wet wash cloth he'd been using for a compress and flopped down on the bed, a picture of despair. "It was a t-third grader! He was a couple inches taller than me, Peter . . . and he's only in the *third grade!*"

"*Bok,*" squawked Niagara Joe, as if he still didn't believe it, and fluttered over to the nightstand.

It was a time a fellow needed a friend.

"Gosh, Duffy," I said, deciding it was useless to ask him what started it. "Does it hurt a lot? I mean, it's been a while since you've had one this bad." I removed the cloth from his eye and took it to the bathroom where I could run more cold water on it.

When I replaced the cloth, Duffy winced. "Peter," he groaned. "I have to find a way to make kids leave me alone!"

"Sure, Duffy," I said, adjusting the cloth slightly so it would stay put. "Like I told you before, it's a matter of self-confidence. You have to act like you don't *care* what people say about your size. That you got bigger things on your mind, you know what I mean?"

Count on me for a poor choice of words.

"I know what you mean," Duffy said huskily. "And that's just the trouble. I don't *have* anything big on my mind. Face the facts, Peter. You're talking to a nobody. I'm the last one chosen for all the games. I'm not a strong enough swimmer to be on the swim team and my only hobby is my plants. Nothing anybody asks about like they ask to see . . . uh, Michael's mechanized robot!"

"What's so great about Michael's robot?" I snorted. "And *I* like your plants, honest! They're . . . interesting."

They *were* interesting, if you took the time to look at them. Duffy had maybe 30 different kinds and he grew almost all of them under fluorescent lights. He needed the lights, which were a special kind, because there wasn't enough sun coming in the window. And not enough space left on the sill, at least not for *his* plants which kept growing and multiplying at a fantastic rate. Duffy sent away for a lot of them—rare ones, he said—and though he didn't talk about it, I knew he was a full fledged member of the American Begonia Society. I saw his membership card, and copies of *The Begonian,* a grown-up kind of magazine only the members receive.

But none of that mattered, because what Duffy said was true. Begonias just didn't score with kids our age, the way a mechanized robot did. And if they were going to stop teasing him, it would take more than a membership in the American Begonia Society to make them do it.

"What I really need is something that'll turn me into a new person," Duffy moaned. "Somebody kids'll respect . . . a person who can do anything he puts his mind to!" He snapped his fingers. "Just like that!" He must have been hurt worse than I thought. He was talking out of his head. I wondered if maybe I should call his aunt and have him checked over for broken bones.

"Oh, come on, Duffy. Nothing'll do that. Lie back now and forget this afternoon. Then, later, if your eye is feeling better, we can watch TV or something. Take your mind off everything that's happened."

It was the wrong thing to say. Niagara Joe cut loose with a torrent of squawks that made it clear what he thought about me and my suggestion. For a bird, he can express himself pretty well. He doesn't talk—for all his trying, Duffy never has been able to teach him that—but he does say *"bok"* and if you are around him long enough, you can guess what he means by the inflection.

Right then, he was telling me to shut up and listen to Duffy.

"Okay, okay," I said, resigned. "Forget I ever mentioned it. You got something in mind you haven't told me about, Duffy?"

Duffy's eyes shone. "It's the answer to all my problems, Peter. Dr. Louis Flamel's Home Study Course in Cosmic Awareness!" He put the compress aside and dropped his voice to a whisper. "I read about it in a magazine. And I'm going to send for it today!"

Swinging his skinny legs over the side of the bed, he reached into the nightstand drawer for a piece of paper. It was a magazine ad he'd been saving and studying for some time. I could tell because it had been folded and re-folded so much the creases were almost worn through.

"Listen, Peter," he said, holding it up to the light. " '*Be everything you desire! Unlock the hidden secrets of the galaxies and bring success and power into your life!*' " As I strained to read over his shoulder, Duffy smoothed out the page on the bed so he could see the fine print. "Here's the best part. '*Instantly, you can have wealth, a dynamic personality, influence! You can control others with your ability to transmit silent commands! You can block your enemies' efforts to hurt you with a centuries-old secret shield of invulnerability!*' Whew! Sounds great, doesn't it, Peter? And it's a 100-percent guaranteed, no-risk offer."

I thought it sounded crazy, but Duffy was pretty excited. His face had lost most of that grayed T-shirt color it had when I came in, and his dark cocker-spaniel eyes glittered like gemstones.

Taking the ad away from him so I could see it, I read through a few more paragraphs, including the one that showed a picture of the founder of the course—Dr. Louis Flamel—posing with a long beard and steel rimmed glasses.

"According to this, Dr. Flamel is the world's leading aura-physicist," I pointed out. "What do you suppose that is?"

Duffy was impatient. "You have to read the whole thing, Peter," he chided and Niagara Joe, putting in his two cents worth, bokked me a good one. "Here . . . this section about cosmic energy fields. You see, Dr. Flamel has spent a lifetime studying them, discovering their secrets and harnessing their power."

It was the part about harnessing cosmic power that appealed the most to Duffy. That, and the part about being invulnerable. To hear him talk, Dr. Flamel's Home Study Course was going to turn him into another Superman, or that other guy we used to see on TV all the time—Steel Man. About the only thing it couldn't do, as far as I could see, was make him taller.

"Oh, I won't care about that," Duffy murmured, forgetting what a big deal it had been to him just hours before. "Once I know the secrets of cosmic awareness, nothing can hurt me! It won't matter how tall I am."

"But, Duffy. . . ."

He ignored me. "Besides, if I send in my order right now, the course will only cost me $7.98, Dr. Flamel's Special Introductory Rate!"

I nearly choked. "$7.98? Duffy, that's a lot of money! Suppose it's just a big gyp? I mean, all that garbage about harnessing the powers of the galaxies and stuff. You don't even know if it'll work!"

Duffy was insulted. "You forget, Peter. Dr. Flamel is a famous scientist. His theories have to work. They're world renowned! And," he added, tossing the ad my way, "there's that 100-percent, no-risk guarantee. It's says so right here!"

He stood up and, limping a little from the clobbering he had taken, he hobbled over to the closet for his floppy felt hat. "Still unconvinced? Well, look at it this way. You can't explain how computers work, but you believe in them, don't you?"

"Yesss. . . ." He had me there. Maybe cosmic awareness was like computers, too complicated for anyone but scientists to understand. And who was I to argue with a scientist?

I wasn't even doing very well with Duffy, because he had already taken out Niagara Joe's Tiny Traveler and was on his way to the door. "Come on, Peter. I want to get a money order and take it to the post office before it closes. Lucky for me Dr. Flamel has his regional headquarters close by. Right down in the city, as a matter of fact. That means I'll get my course in less than a week! Maybe in a couple of days!"

I glanced once more at the ad where it gave the address. "Felicity Sales, Incorporated?" I flared up, noticing it for the first time. "Hold on, Duffy. This doesn't sound like the address of a scientific study center!" A scientific study center is what Dr. Flamel claimed he had. It was supposed to be a kind of clinic, where the weak and troubled went to be restored.

Duffy was unconcerned. "Felicity Sales is probably just his office," he explained. "Use your noodle, Peter. A brilliant researcher like Dr. Flamel doesn't waste time ripping open orders. He needs every minute to study. That's how the secrets of cosmic awareness were discovered in the first place!"

What truth there was to this, I didn't know. But when I finally left Duffy and Joe and checked in at home for supper, I looked up the word "felicity" in the dictionary. It meant anything producing happiness or good fortune.

For Dr. Flamel, maybe that was Duffy's order and his $7.98.

Chapter 2

MY DAD said wait and see. He has this theory sometimes that a person has to learn for himself. Mostly it is when he is discouraged, like when he gets sick of being Grace Gallagher, the newspaper's cooking columnist, and wants to be the author of a best-selling novel, instead.

Actually, my father's real name is Jack Finley, and he is a stub-nosed redhead like me—loaded with freckles—but with a mustache and the rugged, outdoorsy look of one of those old-time fur trappers. It is only because he took this job writing a cooking column, when there wasn't anything else, that he gets letters addressed to Grace Gallagher. The newspaper forwards them to him in a brown envelope. They don't want it known that Grace Gallagher is really a man, either.

In our house, it is kind of a sensitive subject. Not as much as it was when Monica was still around, but touchy enough. Monica was my dad's girlfriend for a while the year I was ten, and though she didn't say anything at first, it got to bug her that my father wasn't the kind of writer she could brag about. So they broke up. And she gave me Dodger, who'd been a present from my dad, but a disappointment to her, because he'd grown too big to fit in her handbag.

Since then, my dad has been working at home, finishing the novel he always meant to write about his army experiences, and writing the Grace Gallagher cooking column which is his regular job. It lets us get by without a full-time housekeeper—the kind who nag at you—and it's neat for other reasons besides. I mean, if I need anything, my dad is always there, cooking or pecking away at his typewriter, and if I want to have a friend over I never have to ask, because it is always okay.

It is okay, for example, that Duffy is sometimes at our place more than he is at his own. My dad, I think, feels a little sorry for him. Through his connections at the newspaper, he knows Captain Smiles. My dad said once that it must have been a real surprise for Captain Smiles to inherit Duffy, though actually it was his wife—Duffy's Aunt Peggy —who did the inheriting. She is Duffy's real mother's sister and his only blood relation. Both his parents died in a Chicago plane crash when he was three.

But all this is only to give you an idea of how things were last summer for Duffy and me. What is really important is what happened when Dr. Flamel's course in cosmic awareness finally arrived.

It was about two weeks later, after school had already let out for vacation, and Duffy had all but given up hope of ever hearing from Felicity Sales or seeing his money again.

I was sitting on the floor teaching Dodger how to roll over for a dog cookie when the doorbell rang and, as usual, Dodger nearly fell apart barking.

"Get that, will you, Peter?" my dad called from the kitchen where he was building a creme-filled strawberry torte for his next week's column. (He always says you "build" something like a torte or a salad; you just "put together" things like bread and casseroles.)

"Okay," I yelled back over the noise and ambled down the front hall after Dodger, who was already at the door.

"Cool it, Dodger!" I ordered sternly. He had just thrown himself feet first at the screen door and was backing up to give it another try. "Who's there? Oh, hi, Duffy."

Standing on the porch, just outside the locked screen, was Duffy and he was wearing as weird a get-up as I've ever seen him in. On his head was his floppy felt hat, but on his back, and hanging almost to his knees, was one of Captain

Smiles' old football jerseys. Because of Duffy's size, it looked more like a nightgown than a shirt, and it had a number 34 on the back and a patch that said "Keep on Truckin'."

"You're out of breath," I commented as I unlatched the door. "Something happen? Like maybe the You Know What came in the mail?"

Duffy smiled mysteriously and put down the shopping bag he was carrying in the front hall. Then, before I had a chance to ask where Niagara Joe was, he reached inside the bag and pulled him out—bokking a string of complaints from the perch of his Tiny Traveler.

"*Woof,*" Dodger barked, lying down at my side with his eyes on Niagara Joe.

He's never made a grab for him, but when it comes to cold facts, Dodger isn't all that crazy about Duffy's budgie. You'd almost think some of Joe's boks were remarks about Dodger's size, the way they upset him. For a Yorkshire Terrier, Dodger is really huge. I mean, most of them weigh around four pounds and are advertised as "tiny teacups." Dodger is more like a coffee mug. He's the biggest Yorkie our vet has ever seen, and sensitive about it, too. I know, because everytime someone mentions his size, he looks ashamed and curls himself up in a ball, so he'll seem smaller.

24

"Hey, Duffy. Ask Joe to quit teasing Dodger," I implored, but he wasn't paying any attention. He was on his knees almost inside his shopping bag, rummaging around for something still at the bottom.

"Tum-te-tah!" He said finally and stood up flourishing a small paperback book. "Look what came today, Peter! *The Secrets of Cosmic Awareness* by Dr. Louis B. Flamel. *'Everything You Need To Know About The Universe To*

Have Wealth, Success and Power Over Those Around You.' "

I peeked inside the shopping bag. "That's not the whole course, is it?" I asked incredulously. "Where's the rest of it?"

Duffy looked embarrassed. "I g-guess that's it, Peter. The mailman brought it to the door and if there'd been anything else he would have given it to me."

I took a quick look at the book which, as far as I could see, didn't even have any pictures. "Duffy, I hate to tell you this, but I think you got gypped. Maybe you should . . . uh, write for your money back. Now, while the guarantee's still good."

Duffy sputtered like a lit firecracker. "It's *not* a gyp!" he insisted, ruffling through the pages and pointing to the headings on chapter after chapter. "You see, Peter? Everything's here! 'How to Have Riches! How to Control Others With Your Thoughts! How to Turn Your Body Into a Dynamic Machine!' Exactly what Dr. Flamel promised. All I have to do is picture what I want and cosmic awareness will turn my mind into a powerful transmitter —directing me to my goal like a giant searchlight and bombarding the obstacles that stand in my way with cosmic energy particles!"

"That's *crazy!*" I yelled. "I don't care *what* Dr. Flamel says. You can't be anything you want just by thinking it! And you can't turn yourself into some kind of . . . transmitter that'll shoot silent commands at people either!"

"Don't be too sure," Duffy snapped, putting his book back inside the shopping bag. "Dr. Flamel said there'd be skeptics like you . . . in his first chapter." His voice cracked and nearly gave up on him in the middle of the sentence. "And I thought you were on my side, Peter. That you wanted me to make a name for myself. Well, some friend *you* are! You won't even give me a chance to prove to you that Dr. Flamel's theories work and that cosmic awareness is everything it claims to be!"

I opened my mouth to object, but Niagara Joe zonked me with a barrage of boks.

"Okay, okay," I surrendered. "I'm sorry, Duffy. Now, why don't we just play . . . uh, Monopoly. I'll even set it up myself and you can have the first turn."

The corners of Duffy's mouth turned up in kind of a tense smile and he gave me a light, friends-again jab on the shoulder. "All right, Peter. I'm game. Niagara Joe's sick of being cooped up anyhow. He needs a chance to stretch his legs."

Maybe that sounds funny to you, a bird stretching his

legs. But for Niagara Joe, who walked almost everywhere he wanted to go, it was exactly right. I think he got a lot of headaches trying to fly. He couldn't get more than a few feet because his wings were clipped, and then he just wound up banging into something.

Niagara Joe played Monopoly though, in his own way. Mostly by picking up the pieces and throwing them around. Or pulling money out from under the edge of the board and biting holes in it.

Dodger, being a dog, had no talent for the game at all, so he just curled up in his bed the minute we took it out.

"There, everything's all set," I said finally and motioned for Duffy, who still looked a little shaky, to join me at the card table. Then, like always, Duffy asked me how many games each of us had won and lost, though why he had to keep a running tally was beyond me. It was something like 42 to 5 in my favor. Too lopsided to keep on recording, in my opinion, particularly when it was just fun we were playing for. Not prizes.

"Duffy," I begged. "Let's not keep track of the games anymore. It's not that important!"

"It *is* important," he insisted, obviously still hurting because I'd knocked Dr. Flamel. "You're just afraid I'll start winning all of a sudden, that's all!"

I watched him straighten his money into neater piles. "Now why'd you want to say a thing like that, Duffy? I *told* you I was sorry. Let's just forget about it and play Monopoly. I don't care *who* wins."

"Well, you better," Duffy warned and let Joe hop from the door of his cage down onto the board. "Because today I'm playing with cosmic awareness and I'm going to beat you. Just see if I don't."

He glared and rolled the dice with a vengeance. "Doubles! That means an extra turn for me, don't forget!"

"I won't forget," I said glumly. Some game it was going to be if he was going to act nasty the whole time. I decided I'd play to win, even though just a minute before I'd considered losing just to cheer Duffy up.

After all, it wasn't entirely his fault that he was gypped by the great Dr. Flamel. It could have happened to anyone. But I guess Duffy wasn't going to admit it. He was going to swallow the whole thing, hook, line and sinker, no matter how dumb it was.

"Ha-*hah!*" He whooped, slapping down his money for Boardwalk the first time around. "My fourth piece of property and one that's going to cost you $2,000 when I get a hotel on it!"

Proudly, Niagara Joe carried the deed around the board

in his beak, then threw it a couple inches into the air so it skittered down and knocked my piece off its place.

"Hey, watch it," I said testily. "Now, where was I? Duffy, Niagara Joe has to be more careful!"

Duffy smiled. He was staring at me in kind of a strange way like he was counting each and every freckle on my face.

"Shake the dice, Peter."

I did, and wound up in jail.

"Bok," squawked Niagara Joe, waddling over to my side of the board where he began pulling out my money.

"Stop him!" I shouted so loud that Dodger sat up in his bed, alert. "He's messing everything up!"

Ordinarily, it was kind of fun having Duffy's budgie playing Monopoly with us. But that day, he was a pain in the neck.

When I got out of jail, Duffy already had a hotel which I would have missed if Niagara Joe hadn't been playing with the dice. I shook what looked like an eight, but he picked them up and I had to shake again. Eleven.

The next thing you know, Duffy's collecting $1,100.

"I told you I was going to win," he said, smugly.

"You wouldn't be if it weren't for that bird," I growled, wishing Duffy would quit staring at me. "He's a nuisance! I can't keep my mind on my game."

"Hah!" Duffy said and threw doubles for the tenth time that afternoon.

It was the worst run of luck that I'd had in a year. But it wasn't all that. I was making some stupid mistakes, too—not buying up property when I should have—while Duffy was playing like a junior J. Paul Getty.

The final blow came when I was down to $200 in cash and all the houses that I had owned were back at the bank. I was on Water Works hoping for a twelve to get me safely past Duffy's biggies.

Before I could shake, Niagara Joe bokked and kicked over the Chance cards. Straightened up again, they would have been okay, but he went one step further and picked up the top one in his beak.

"Hey, look," Duffy said. " *'Take a ride on the Reading. If you pass go, collect $200.'* "

"Put it on the bottom," I grumbled. "There's no point leaving it on top now. We both know what it is."

The next minute I was wishing I'd kept my mouth shut. I rolled an eight that put me right on the Chance space between the Short Line and Park Place.

"Well, you got past my hotel on Pennsylvania Avenue," Duffy commented, as I picked up the card on top of the Chance pile.

"Take a walk on the Boardwalk," I groaned. *"Advance token to Boardwalk."*

"Way to go!" Duffy shouted, and we both knew it was the end of the game. "With the hotel, you owe me exactly $2,000! Pretty good for a former Nobody, eh, Peter?"

"It was your stupid bird that kept me from playing my best game," I complained afterwards.

"You're full of beans," Duffy contradicted me enthusiastically. "If you want to know the truth, it was Dr. Flamel's Secrets of Cosmic Awareness in action. I just pictured you losing and me winning. And it worked! I hated to do it to you, Peter, but those cosmic energy particles of mine had you beaten before you even started."

I thought back to those trance-like stares he'd been zinging at me all through the game. Was it possible?

Then I glanced at Niagara Joe, who was still on the Monopoly board.

"Bok," he squawked and turned over a Community Chest card that said *"Get out of jail free."*

Chapter 3

THERE'S THIS thing about being friends that says you can't blame a guy for believing what he wants to, even if you, yourself, think it's nuts. Like Duffy ignoring the part Niagara Joe played in our Monopoly game and deciding instead that it was cosmic awareness that helped him.

I'll admit there was a chance that it had, but a pretty slim one. Duffy, however, was convinced and so stubborn about it that I got bugged and didn't call him for two days. Then I got tired of being by myself and shuffled over to the Randalls' apartment to see how he was getting on.

"You'll find him in his room," Captain Smiles greeted me, "turning his body into a dynamic machine."

"A dynamic machine?" I blurted out. "How's he going to do that?"

"Don't ask me," scoffed Duffy's uncle. "I offered to send him to a gym, but he's doing some kind of exercise he heard about on his own."

There was a puzzled look on his face. "Nothing like I've ever seen before, that's for sure. Too . . . mystical. And if you ask me, absolutely worthless. The kid needs regular workouts. The same kind I do."

He jogged a bit in place to show me what he meant, but he didn't have time to demonstrate the other exercises. His staff at the TV station was waiting for him. They had a show to plan and he was late already.

I wished him luck and went to find Duffy, who was seated on the floor in the center of his room.

"Hi, Duffy. What are you doing?"

His legs were out straight, his shoes off, and his arms up in the air in front of him. "I'm following Dr. Flamel's prescription for muscles of steel."

"How? By doing sit-ups?"

"No, by concentrating, breathing properly . . . a lot of stuff," he said between clenched teeth. Then he sucked in a deep breath, held it while he raised his arms above his head, and exhaled as he leaned forward and grabbed his toes. Joe, who'd been picking at the laces in Duffy's shoe, bokked and fluttered away.

"Uhnn. It's supposed to sound like air rushing out of a balloon," Duffy croaked, his face red. "Uncle Ralph says I'll never get anyplace with an exercise like this, but I know better. What do you think, Peter? I've been at this for a couple of days now. Do you notice any change?"

I gave him the once over. "You don't *look* any different," I said honestly. "How do you feel?"

Duffy stood up and flexed his muscles. "I *feel* like a new kid. Like every muscle in my body is as strong as a steel cable, you know what I mean?" He sauntered over to the mirror on his closet door and studied his image carefully. "In my mind, I have this picture of my body as a dynamic machine that'll do anything I command it to do, and the more I concentrate on it, the faster cosmic awareness makes it so."

We were back talking about tiny energy particles which was not my idea of a fun morning.

For one thing, I couldn't see Duffy as a dynamic machine, no matter what he said. It was like Dodger pretending to be a tiny teacup.

"Duffy, don't get me wrong now, I think it's great that you're exercising your muscles and stuff, but I don't think *anybody* has the kind of body you're talking about. You'd have to be a . . . robot! Some kind of *superman!*"

Duffy scowled. "There you go again, Peter, trying to be an authority on something you know nothing about. Dr. Flamel says a person can be anything he desires through cosmic awareness. He just has to. . . ."

"I know, I know. *Picture it!* Duffy, that's like me deciding I want to grow another head . . . one without freckles. I could *think* about it from here till doomsday, but I'd still wind up with the one I have!"

Duffy didn't seem to care. He just closed the conversation with another deep breath and picked up Niagara Joe who'd been waiting for him on top of the plant light.

"Let's not fight anymore, Peter. I have to go to the library for this plant book they're saving for me, and now that you're here, maybe you can go with me. We can have lunch afterwards—your famous eggs or cold spaghetti, if you'd rather. My Aunt Peggy's not going to be home, so she won't care."

Hooked as I was on cold spaghetti and my own invention, reversible eggs, which were scrambled on top and fried on the bottom, I had to turn Duffy down. "I have a one o'clock dentist appointment," I explained regretfully. "But I can run over to the library. Do you mind walking? My bike's got a bent wheel, and my dad won't be able to fix it till this afternoon."

Duffy was already putting on his hat. "No sweat," he said hoarsely, then coaxed Joe into his Tiny Traveler. "But let's move. I'm anxious to get out into the air and get my gears meshing. When your body's a machine that'll do anything you command it to do, you can't let it sit idle."

"Guess not," I muttered, but Duffy didn't hear me. He was halfway down the hall, his pistons driving and his engine racing along at top speed.

It was only later—after we'd picked up his book on herbs and a couple others he'd found on lawn and garden care—that he began to slow down.

"Makes you hungry, huh?" I remarked, as he lingered in front of a sandwich shop window.

Niagara Joe took the opportunity to enjoy a few seeds.

"Hungry?" Duffy groaned. "I'm starving. I only had a cupcake for breakfast this morning and then I got right at my exercises."

"Well," I said, wishing there was time to stop for a pizza slice, "we'll be home soon and then you can fix yourself a sandwich. You probably use up a lot of extra energy doing all those sit-ups and stuff, Duffy. No wonder you're hungry!"

We ambled down the street for still another block, then crossed over to Forrest Avenue where it was a lot shadier. It was there that Duffy spotted this old lady trying to build a rock wall planter single-handedly in her front yard. She wasn't a big woman, but she had this set to her jaw that gave you the impression that she did this kind of thing all the time.

"Hey, Peter, stop for a minute. She's got some lavender over there in her garden and I want to ask here where she bought it."

It was a good thing he did, because the next thing you know, the lady began to look dizzy and we had to help her sit down on a lawn chair under a tree.

"Why do you want to build a stone thing like this by yourself, anyway?" I asked, after getting her a drink of water. "You ought to hire a handyman. Or a couple of big teenagers. This is heavy work."

The old woman's jaw jutted out even more. "Try to get someone who'll do it the way you want . . . or at a price you can afford. I'm on a pension. When I want something done, I just do it myself."

"Haven't you got a son?" Duffy asked. "Or a nephew?"

"Not one that'd lift a finger for me," she said unhappily. "Too busy with their own projects. 'Be over to do it soon,

Mother,' they keep on saying. Well, I'm not waiting any longer. I'm doing it myself!"

Duffy scratched his head and eyed the wheelbarrow and the pile of rocks. Then he pulled me to one side.

"Peter?"

"Look, Duffy," I said, before he could finish. "I've got this dentist appointment. Tomorrow, we can come back here and help her, if she wants. Today, I just can't do it."

The old lady overheard us talking. "Oh, don't you boys worry about a thing. Just go ahead, I'll finish on my own. In a few minutes . . . after I rest some."

Duffy wouldn't hear of it. Maybe it was because he didn't have a mother or grandmother of his own, or maybe because she fancied herbs like him, but he offered to do the whole job for her by himself. For whatever she wanted to pay.

"Duffy," I protested, as he handed me Joe and his stack of plant books. "This is no job for a kid!" I wanted to add, a kid his size. "Ask her to wait till tomorrow. Then we'll try to do it together."

Duffy didn't want to wait. "You forget, Peter. I'm trained for this kind of task. Hard as it may look, cosmic awareness will make it easy for me. Dr. Flamel promised, so it's a scientific fact."

Scientific fact or not, I thought it was a poor plan. There was a good reason why the old lady's nephews and sons were slow coming to help her, and a good reason why she couldn't hire anyone, either. Some of the rocks in the pile were the size of watermelons. It would take more strength than Duffy had to lift them, even with the help of his energy particles.

Well, what happened was I took Joe and Duffy's books back to my place while Duffy stayed to begin work on the rock wall.

"I (mumph) told him I'd be back to help later," I said to my dad through a meat and lettuce sandwich. "When I finish with the (mumph) dentist, and wherever else we have to go."

I don't think my dad really heard, because he just kept saying "uh-huh" and staring at the paper in his typewriter. It was a new thing to him, writing a novel. And it took a lot more concentration than building a creme-filled strawberry torte, or putting together a Grace Gallagher cookbook. So he never realized what a man-sized job Duffy had taken on, or he might have stopped it.

As it was, nobody stopped it, and I—like the world's prize dummy—didn't even remember that Duffy might miss lunch until it was too late.

I hadn't actually promised to bring him one, but I could have offered. He wasn't likely to get lunch on the job. The lady probably wouldn't realize he was going without it, and Duffy would be too embarrassed to ask for something himself.

So I took along a couple of candy bars when I ran back to help him later.

By that time, Duffy was just hefting the last rocks in place. Considering how the ground was torn up around the planter, it looked like he'd had to drag some of them into

position—the ones that were too heavy to lift or even tip into the wheelbarrow.

"Duffy! I'm here! Let me help."

He pushed back his bangs and the sweat and dirt rolled down his face. "Uhnnn. Hi, Peter."

I shoved him to one side so I could get my hands back of the rock he was tipping end over end. "Duffy, why don't you sit down? Have one of these candy bars. I'll finish. I'm just sorry I didn't get here sooner."

He had a funny look about him—kind of glassy eyed, if you know what I mean. And he was flushed.

The old lady was still sitting in the shade, supervising his work. She had a pitcher of lemonade on a little table nearby, so she'd obviously given Duffy something, but I didn't think it was a meat and lettuce sandwich. Not the way Duffy was tottering around. There wasn't enough zip left in him to tear open a candy wrapper, so I did it for him and held it till he took the first bite.

I don't think he even knew what he was eating.

"Just . . . two . . . more . . . rocks . . . to . . . go," he choked and rubbed at his back like it was going to cave in on him any second. Difficult as it was for him to talk, there was still a certain amount of pride in his voice. "I did it, Peter, didn't I?" he kept saying. "Like . . . a . . . dy-namic . . . machine."

"Sure, Duffy," I said, half wondering if there was something to cosmic awareness after all. "You have muscles of steel. But give 'em a rest now. Sit down over there for a minute and then we'll go home."

It was that minute rest that really finished Duffy off. Once his muscles got the message they could stop working, they gave up entirely. When the lady saw how tired he was, she insisted he go home, too—after telling him what a fine job he'd done and giving him two dollars from her purse.

Duffy just smiled weakly. He had about as much strength as a wet noodle when I hauled him through the apartment door.

His Aunt Peggy must have thought he'd fallen out of a tree or something, because she took one look and nearly went to pieces. She'd just arrived herself a little earlier and found him missing, so she was worried. Later, after she'd put him to bed and called the doctor, she calmed down some, and it was then that I went home to get Duffy's books and Niagara Joe, who was probably miserable without him.

When I returned, after supper, Captain Smiles was there having a late dinner on a tray in front of the tube.

"Hey, thanks for bringing back Duffy's gear," he said with a little wave of his salad fork. "You'll find him in bed. Bushed, I guess. Don't know what he was trying to prove. A few weirdo exercises and he thinks he's a strong man.

I *told* him. Regular workouts, it's the only way!"

Niagara Joe bokked and I hustled him down the hall to Duffy's room.

"Look who's here," I said softly, as I took Joe out of the Tiny Traveler and set him on Duffy's bed. "Duffy? It's me, Peter. And Niagara Joe. Are you awake?"

Duffy opened his eyes and spoke in a sleepy whisper. "I did it, Peter. Didn't I? I . . . can . . . do . . . anything . . . I . . . want . . . to . . . do."

"Sure, Duffy," I said again and tucked the sheet a little closer under his chin.

Then I put Niagara Joe back in his regular cage. The dynamic machine was asleep and for all I knew, he would sleep for a couple of days.

What he'd do when he woke up, though, had me worried. Dr. Flamel had Duffy convinced he was indestructible. And trying to be something he was never meant to be, even with cosmic awareness.

Chapter 4

MY DAD had his own thoughts about Duffy's efforts to become superkid. And about Captain Smiles, whom he felt was responsible for at least part of it.

"If he'd just forget for a day that he once played defensive tackle for the Chicago Bears, things might be different. He'd quit giving Duffy the impression that being small is something to be ashamed of. Then, hopefully, he'd wake up to some of Duffy's real talents."

There was some truth to what my dad said. I'd seen Captain Smiles' football trophies myself. But whether he'd ever care about Duffy's real talents, I wasn't sure. Being good with plants was a lot different from being All-American. I knew that raising them was special, but—like Duffy said —it didn't make it for him with the rest of the kids. So probably, it'd never mean anything to Captain Smiles, either. It sure hadn't so far.

I was just thinking maybe I should work out with Duffy more—catching passes, perhaps—when he showed up at the back door with Niagara Joe.

"Hey, I was just going to call you," I said, jumping up to let him in. "Want to go out back and toss around a football?"

Duffy shook his head. "Some other time, Peter. Right now, I have something important on my mind, something that'll mean a lot to both of us if we can just get it underway."

In his opinion, he'd fulfilled his desire to become a dynamic machine and was half through Dr. Flamel's chapter on how to be rich.

"You're going to open your own business?" I gasped, surprised.

"That's right. And since you're my best friend, I want you to be my partner." He put Joe down on the kitchen table and took a doughnut from the freshly made batch I offered him.

My dad had gone into the den to answer some of his fan mail, and Dodger was sitting on the chair next to me, sharing my doughnut.

"Suppose I don't want to be a partner? Look, Duffy," I began, wishing he would stop with these crazy ideas. "You know what the situation is like in this neighborhood. Don't get me wrong. I think it's great that you want to earn money doing odd jobs for people. I'd like to, too. But face it, those kids who run *Help Is Here* aren't going to like someone muscling in on their territory."

Actually, it was one kid who ran the *Help Is Here* organization. The others were just sort of employees. When the jobs came in, they took the ones they were best at, then turned back part of what they were paid to the organization. Which, of course, was this kid who thought up the idea in the first place, who advertised in all the supermarkets and on telephone poles and parceled out the calls as they came in.

Knowing what a big business it was, I had tried to sign up for it myself earlier in the year, but the boy I talked to about the job said I was too young. It was just for junior high school kids, he said. He wouldn't even tell me the name of the kid who ran it so I could go straight to the top.

Finally, I gave up and satisfied myself with a sometime job I have mowing our neighbors' lawn and shoveling their driveway in the winter. Not a big money maker, but fairly steady.

"So you see, Duffy? They don't even want kids our age *applying* to them for jobs. If you go one step further and try to take work *away* from them, you'll get clobbered!"

I bit into my third doughnut. It was a fair piece of advice for anyone with a mind to listen. And for a kid the size of Duffy, it was more than that. It was a warning. I respected the *Help Is Here* bunch a whole lot, myself. And for good reason. They were bigger than me, and I didn't want to tangle with them.

But Duffy?

"Peter, you're forgetting I know how to get what I want. You saw how I beat you at . . . uh, how I moved all those rocks single-handed. I'm a new person now. I can. . . ."

"Hold it, Duffy."

"No, let me finish. There's plenty of room in this neighborhood for two odd-job companies. You believe in free enterprise, don't you? Besides," he continued, reaching in his pocket for a pencil and paper, "my business is going to be different. I'm going to specialize in jobs that are too tough for anyone else. Jobs that require a certain kind of rare talent, get what I mean?"

I was afraid I did, although I didn't like to think about it.

"You mean you're going to call on your cosmic energy particles again. And you think they'll help you do all these jobs? The ones that are too tough for anyone else?"

It was crazy. But Duffy felt differently.

"Peter, there you go again acting like a skeptic. Just *believe* I can do it and help me get some flyers ready telling people we're available. After all, *I'm* not worried what the *Help Is Here* gang'll do to us. You shouldn't be either."

"But, Duffy," I pleaded. "There are at least twenty-five of them, not counting whoever runs the thing. Erghhh . . ." I shuddered. "You've seen how big some of those kids are. Imagine what the one at the top is like."

"Never fear, Peter," Duffy answered and held up a sample of the advertising flyer he wanted me to see. "I'll just picture them vanquished and my cosmic awareness will do the rest."

Niagara Joe bokked.

"For cripes' sake, Duffy!"

"It's true, Peter. When I put my mind to it, my energy field is so strong that not even my strongest enemy can penetrate it."

I sighed and wiped the sweat from my forehead. "Okay, let's see the flyer. You planning to make these up by hand?

Help Is Here had theirs done at one of those Instant Print places. That's why there are so many around, I guess. But it costs money."

Duffy seemed unconcerned and turned over his masterpiece.

GOT A PROBLEM?

NO JOB'S TOO TOUGH FOR DUFFY MOON, INC.

LET ME HANDLE THAT CHORE THAT NO ONE ELSE WILL TOUCH.

A COMPLETELY NEW, ALTOGETHER SECRET METHOD I HAVE AT

MY DISPOSAL PERMITS ME TO DO . . . ANYTHING!

REASONABLE RATES.

DON'T WAIT!   CALL NOW!

SUGARBUSH 8-5324

"Hey, wait a minute," I yelped. "That's *my* phone number!"

"I know," Duffy replied, his voice cracking. "You're going to be my partner, aren't you? I thought we could take all the calls here, so we won't bother my aunt."

"What about my dad?" I countered, glad he was not in the same room. "Just because he's home all day doesn't mean he's not working." My dad says writers have this problem all the time. The PTA can't understand, for example, why he won't be a room mother.

50

"Besides, I never promised I'd *be* your partner, Duffy. I'm still in one piece and I'd like to stay that way. What *you* want is up to you."

Duffy looked stricken.

"Oh, I'll help you deliver the flyers, I guess. I can do that much. But count me out of the rest of it. And take our phone number off the ad."

"I sure am glad you understand about me not wanting to be your partner," I told Duffy two days later as we were tucking flyers into all the mailboxes on our block. "After all, it's nothing personal. I really mean it when I say I hope you're successful. I'd like to see you get all the jobs you can handle . . . and without any trouble either, if you know what I mean."

Things were already off to an astonishing start. For a kid who'd called himself a nothing just a few weeks before, I had to hand it to him. With the two dollars the old lady had given him for building her planter and this thing he called cosmic awareness, he'd talked a quick print place into running off 100 flyers—on credit! With the promise, of course, that he'd pay them back with the money he earned from his next job.

It could have been cosmic energy that turned the trick,

though I'm not sure. Mostly, I think it was Duffy's new and absolute certainty that he could not fail. The man at the print shop took notice of it, anyway. He was so impressed that, when the talk got around to Duffy's secret method, he didn't even insist on knowing what it was. If a secret wasn't a secret, he said, how could it grab the customers when they opened their mailboxes?

It wouldn't if we didn't get all the flyers delivered.

"Duffy? How many more have you got? I still have about ten."

"About the same. You want to stop, Peter? I can deliver the rest tomorrow."

"Nah, I'll finish." It was slow work, but I didn't want to complain because we were going to play street hockey afterwards. It was our favorite game—after Monopoly—and we played it almost year 'round, until it snowed. Since we usually had the game down at Duffy's, on one of the apartment courtyards, I'd brought along my hockey stick, though Duffy planned to run in and get his later, when we were through with our deliveries.

He wasn't saying much and I had the feeling that, like me, he was keeping his eye out for the *Help Is Here* gang. We hadn't seen any of them around that afternoon, which wasn't normal, and it was beginning to put me on edge. Very much on edge.

"Hey, Duffy?"

"Yeah, Peter?"

"You see someone sneak around that garage up ahead? I thought it looked like a kid I know. The one that put me down when I asked him for a job with *Help Is Here*."

Duffy bit his lip some, but he didn't suggest we turn back; he didn't even slow down his steps which, in my opinion, should have stopped right there.

It didn't matter. The kid I'd met from *Help Is Here* came out to greet us. Like a lot of kids with braces, he had an occasional lisp, but it was a real tough one and I don't think anyone bothered him because of it.

"Okay, th-top right there, thrimp," he growled at Duffy, who still had the flyers in his hand. "Don't you know all the jobs in thith area are taken care of by *Help Is Here?*"

He'd obviously picked up a copy of Duffy's ad somewhere along our route. It was sticking out of his back pocket; at least it was until he whipped it out and shoved it under Duffy's nose.

"*Runt,* you weren't *thinking* when you th-tarted to pass these out!"

"Now, just a minute," I objected, trying to prevent what was almost sure to happen.

I could have saved my breath. Instead of turning red, Duffy just stood his ground, calmly, his spaniel eyes fixed in this trance-like stare. It was almost like he'd lost consciousness and the *Help Is Here* kid didn't know what to make of him. Then he laughed and grabbed Duffy by the shirt and lifted him off the ground.

"Duffy?" There was still a way out, I figured, but a slim one. Duffy could promise to take back every one of the flyers. In fact, I'd even help him.

I underestimated the new certainty he had that he was indestructible. Even being held up in the air like that, he didn't flinch. He just looked his attacker square in the eye and said nothing, although I saw his lips move once or twice like he was talking under his breath.

"You th-aying something, tiger?" the kid wanted to know. "Out with it! Or are you too th-cared?" He laughed.

"Duffy's not afraid and neither am I," I said, getting a good grip on my hockey stick and moving it out front where he could see it. "Better put him down. Or you'll be sorry."

The big kid looked first at me, then at the hockey stick, then back at me. "Hey, you're Peter Finley, aren't you?" he sputtered, loosening his hold on Duffy. "The one who asked me for a job? You part of this *Duffy Moon, Inc.,* too?"

I hesitated, swallowing hard.

"I'm . . . uh, his business manager," I said, trying to make my eyes go steely.

There was the hockey stick, I kept telling myself; it

would give us the advantage for a time. Like maybe five minutes. Maybe even a little more if I was fast on my feet.

Duffy spoke up at last. "We're *partners,* right, Peter?"

I gripped the hockey stick tighter. "Yeah."

Our opponent thought this over. "Well, I'm . . . uh, under orders not to do anything to you now," he explained, saving face. "Because the Big Boss is away on vacation. But, take thith piece of advice. *Help Is Here* doesn't like competition. So fold up shop now before it'th too late!"

"Who's the Big Boss?" Duffy yelled after him as he loped down the street.

"Boots McAfee!" the kid hollered back. *"And they don't come any tougher!"*

"Boy, that was a close one," I said, sitting down on the step and wiping my brow. "Look at m-me. I'm s-still shaking."

Duffy pulled himself up to his full height and looked triumphant. "I wasn't really worried. I knew cosmic awareness would see us through. I just pictured that bully running from us in fear and he did. It worked perfectly!"

I flexed the fingers in my hand that were still sore from wielding the hockey stick. Should I hit him with it? On the other hand, suppose he was right?

"Glad after all this time you decided to be my partner,"

56

Duffy added, reaching out his hand.

I shook it. "Might as well," I mumbled weakly. "Though why I said I would when I promised myself I wouldn't is beyond me."

Duffy smiled mysteriously. "It isn't beyond me," he said, and I had a feeling that I'd been zonked by something I didn't even believe in . . . cosmic power.

Chapter 5

"SO WHO'S Boots McAfee?" I asked Duffy that night as he hunched on our front steps and I worked over Dodger's matted coat with a hairbrush.

"Beats me," Duffy said, his chin in his hands. "Some junior high school kid, I guess. But it sure isn't anyone who went to our school or we'd remember."

"Not necessarily. But you could be right. Chances are he went to Stony Brook or one of the others. Maybe even the Academy."

I rolled Dodger over and brushed the long hair under his muzzle. "Did you check the phone book?"

"Sure, and I think he lives over on Fairchild. But what good does that do? He's not home and I don't know anyone over there who can tell us anything about him."

"We could ask around," I suggested, fighting Dodger for the brush. Then I thought over what I'd just said. "No, maybe it's best we stay out of that neighborhood entirely. We might question the wrong people. Or we might find out that he's six feet tall and is the wrestling champion at the high school."

Duffy stared out into the darkness. "You sound worried, Peter. Don't be. My cosmic awareness will protect us both. It worked on that other kid, didn't it? Well, it'll work on Boots McAfee, too. Take my word for it."

I put the finishing touches on Dodger's topknot and stood up. It was useless to argue with Duffy over what I was sure really scared away our first opponent. But I didn't want him taking things for granted. The next time I might not have my hockey stick. And Boots McAfee might show up with the entire *Help Is Here* gang.

"Duffy? Don't push those . . . uh, cosmic energy particles too far. They might not be strong enough to take care of a character like Boots. He sounds like a pretty tough cookie. Maybe he has his own magic!"

I was wondering if there was an easier way to get rich. That would be less hazardous.

But Duffy didn't want to join me in thinking of one. He was determined to make a name for himself as the president of *Duffy Moon, Inc.,* and he believed he had cosmic awareness behind him all the way.

Three days later, though, he was still just a nobody. Without a job, or even a prospect.

"I can't understand it, Peter. We distributed nearly one hundred flyers."

It bothered him that there weren't a hundred phone calls the first day. There wasn't one, if you really want to know the truth. Not on the first day, or even the second.

The morning we were hanging from the apartment jungle gym, though, was a different story.

"Duf-fy?" His Aunt Peggy called from the wrought iron balcony they have off their dining room. "There's a telephone call for you . . . and Peter. Can you come up and get it?"

"Be right there," Duffy yelled back, then turned to me with raised eyebrows. "Whoever it is asked for you, too," he whispered hoarsely. "Do you suppose it could be a customer?"

I really didn't see how it could be, since my name wasn't on the flyer, but there was nothing to do but find out. Word of me being Duffy's business manager might have gotten around. In spite of me wishing, without hope, I guess, that it would stay a secret.

Anyway, like Duffy figured, the call did turn out to be a customer. A Mrs. Varner, who lives across the street from my dad and me. She has two little boys—Andrew and Brian—and she needed someone to babysit with them.

"She sounds kind of desperate," Duffy croaked, holding his hand over the mouthpiece of the phone. "Can you go over there with me this afternoon?"

I hesitated. "To babysit? Duffy, we don't know anything about babysitting. We don't even have little brothers!"

Duffy hissed at me to be quiet. "Never mind that. Can you go? It's our first customer, Peter. I can't turn her down."

"Okay, but if we blow it, don't say I didn't warn you. You never told me we'd be *babysitting*. I thought we were going to mow lawns and stuff and tackle those jobs that are too tough for anyone else."

Duffy shrugged and returned to Mrs. Varner who was still on the line. Like a true student of cosmic awareness, he didn't have the doubts that I did. He was so sure we'd be a big success that he even brought along Niagara Joe to share in the glory. Joe was between us in an A & P grocery bag as we rang the bell, and I held my breath for fear he would bok at Mrs. Varner when she opened the door.

He just made a peep that she didn't even notice.

"Oh, come in, come in," she said, breathing what sounded like a sigh of relief. "I'm so happy you're here. When I couldn't get any of my regular sitters—not even *Help Is Here* would come—I thought of you, Peter. Then your father told me you were over at your friend's, so I called there."

She eyed Duffy. "I didn't realize that he was so much younger than you, though. Are you sure he . . . uh, won't be in the way?"

Duffy colored slightly and pulled himself up to his full height.

"Duffy's the same age as me, Mrs. Varner," I said. "And he's president of our company, *Duffy Moon, Inc.*"

Mrs. Varner apologized, but she looked so confused that I didn't really relax till she reached for her purse and gloves.

"Well, then. I must say I appreciate you coming over on such short notice. And the fact that there are *two* of you is . . . uh, ideal. One of you for each of *them,* if you know what I mean."

Not having had much contact with her two boys before, I wasn't sure what she *did* mean, but it made me a little uncomfortable.

Still, the puzzling thing on my mind at that point was not the boys, but why she had called us. "You didn't get the phone number off the flyer?" I asked, as Duffy, who didn't seem to care where she got it, wandered into the next room to inspect her house plants.

Mrs. Varner took the car keys from her handbag. "Flyer? What flyer? I told you, Peter, I called your dad and he said you were over at Duffy's. Now, Brian's playing with his trucks in the nursery, but . . . uh, Andrew's under the bed and he won't come out."

"Won't come out?" Duffy looked up, a potted plant in his hand.

Mrs. Varner was embarrassed. "Oh, I'm sure he will in a minute or two. He usually does. It's just that . . . well, he doesn't like to see me go. But with you boys here to play with him, everything will be just fine."

She went to the stairs. "Andrew? Brian? I'm going now, sweethearts. Be good! I'll be home again in a couple of hours."

"Duffy," I said, when I shut the door behind her, "she never even *looked* at the flyer we left. Doesn't that worry you? What if nobody else read their flyer, either? Or worse, what if *Help Is Here* went around and collected all of them right after we finished?"

Duffy put the plant down and picked off a dead leaf. "The flyers went in with the mail and no one can tamper with that, Peter. Don't be such a worrier. The jobs are starting to come in, aren't they?" He smiled and took Niagara Joe's cage from the bag.

"One of them did, but . . ."

"More of them will! In a week, we'll be legends in our own time. Come on now, let's find the boys. I want to try out my cosmic awareness on Andrew, the one she said was under the bed."

I followed Duffy uncertainly, my mind still boggled by the possibility that we'd been sabotaged.

It didn't take me long to realize we'd been trapped instead. By Mrs. Varner, who was probably miles away, enjoying her freedom.

Upstairs, in Andrew's room, Brian, who was about two, was coloring on the wall. Andrew, the older of the two by a few years, was still under the bed.

Not knowing how a real babysitter would handle things, I reacted instinctively. I took the crayon away from Brian, who just stared and toddled back to the box for another. Then I lifted the corner of the bedspread and with more courtesy, introduced myself to Andrew.

I could have saved my breath.

"An-drew," I tried again, this time with what I figured was a more professional approach. "Come see what your brother has done to your wall. It's really colorful."

There was silence from under the bed.

"Andrew?"

I saw something move and wheeled around just in time to grab a black crayon from Brian, who giggled and pulled himself into a chair.

"Hey, kid!" I yelled, as he reached for the dresser lamp. "Everything up here's a no-no. Duffy, what are you *doing,* anyway? Aren't you going to give me a hand?"

Like some Indian guru in a trance, Duffy was sitting cross-legged on the floor with Niagara Joe, breathing heavily. "Shhh," he whispered between breaths. "I'm trying to get through to Andrew's mind with my cosmic power. Can't you almost feel it? Millions of tiny energy particles lining themselves up into one powerful beam!"

I gritted my teeth. The only think I could feel at that moment was Brian squirming out of my grasp.

"Buhd! Buhd!" he shrieked and pointed. He'd caught sight of poor Niagara Joe, who was eyeing him warily.

"Take it easy, Brian," I said, holding him down. "You can see the bird in a minute after my friend works his magic on your brother."

I was being sarcastic, but the kids didn't know that.

There was a slight stir under the bed and Brian struggled harder.

"You don't understand, do you?" I said, trying to be con-

versational when what I really wanted to do was throttle Duffy. "My partner, the babysitting expert, has these rare magical powers, Brian. That's why he's sitting there with his eyes shut, puffing up like a balloon."

Duffy exhaled loudly and Niagara Joe bokked.

"Bloon?" Brian asked, recognizing a familiar word. *"Bloon?"*

I nodded. Then there was a *creakk!* The bed trembled a

little and the next thing I saw was Andrew's head peeping out from under the bedspread.

It was Duffy he was staring at. And no wonder. Hearing him breathe and then seeing him there on the floor with a live bird was too much, even for Andrew.

"It's Dr. Small!" he whispered in awe, then directed a question at me. "Can he make me teeny-tiny?"

I was too surprised to talk.

The bed groaned and Andrew slid out from under it and stood up, clearly impatient for an answer. "You said he's *magic!* Can he make me teeny-tiny so I can fly around on that bird?"

Andrew was obviously a fan of "Super Crow and Dr. Small"—a brand-new Saturday morning cartoon series about a vet who gets animals out of all kinds of predicaments by making himself small and flying around on his crow.

"I don't know. Duffy? Andrew's out. And he has a question for you."

Duffy blinked. "My beams of thought power have reached their target," he droned and began to breathe normally. "I . . . am . . . now . . . coming . . . out . . . of . . . my . . . trance."

I let go of Brian. "Great. Now all you have to do is make

Andrew tiny enough to fly around on Niagara Joe's back and the afternoon will be a big success!"

"Dr. Small giving take-off instructions to Super Crow!" Andrew lisped, bending down over Joe's cage and looking him square in the eye.

Brian did him one better. He ran over to Niagara Joe and began jabbing at him through the bars of the cage with a Tinker Toy.

"Bok!" squawked Niagara Joe, terrified.

"Cut it out, you kids," Duffy said sharply.

Then he stood up, with Joe's tiny cage under his arm where it would be out of reach, and stroked his chin, Dr. Flamel style.

"Sorry, Andrew and Brian. Super Crow and I only make people small on . . . uh, Wednesdays. Today is Thursday."

Andrew didn't understand.

"He's saying he can't make you teeny-tiny today," I explained, giving Duffy a dirty look. "Some other day. Now, why don't we go get your trucks and play filling station."

"Noo!" Andrew screamed, finally getting the message. "I don't want to play station. I want to fly around on Super Crow like Dr. Small does on TV."

I groaned and buried my face in my hands. "Okay,

Duffy, you take it from here. You know all the secrets of the universe. Use one of them."

For a second, he just stood there thinking. Then he said, "How'd you like to be a frog, instead, Andrew? We can do that today. Look!"

I blinked and there was Duffy, hopping around on the floor in a frog-like crouch, Niagara Joe still tucked under one arm close to his chest.

"*Gleep*," he croaked in his deep voice and the boys laughed delightedly.

"*Guh-leep, guh-leep*," Andrew imitated quickly and squatted down on the floor beside him.

It was a neat idea, particularly on the spur of the moment. And after a few tries, we had little Brian doing it, too. Then the trouble started. Andrew wouldn't stop.

"*Guh-leep!*" he croaked over a half hour later when Duffy suggested it was time to play something else.

"*Guh-leep!*" he garumphed when we tried to get him to come down to the rec room with us where there were more toys.

"Duf-fy!" I said, studying Andrew who was squatting comfortably by my side. "Make him quit. It isn't as if you really *changed* him into a frog. It was just a game!"

Duffy bent over, friendly-like, and tried to talk sense to

Andrew. "Frog time's over now," he said, waving his arms. "See? I've turned you back into a *boy*. Now we can all play trucks."

Andrew took a hop toward the door, a smile of contentment on his face. *"Guh-leep,"* he croaked and looked back. *"Gleep!"*

"Duffy!" Mrs. Varner was due home soon and it would take some rehearsing to know what to say. Maybe: it was great babysitting for you, Mrs. Varner, but we accidentally turned one of your boys into a frog?

Not that I really believed Andrew *was* a frog, you understand. It was just that, well, face it—coming home to a kid who *thought* he was one might be pretty upsetting. Especially for Mrs. Varner, who would have been happy just getting Andrew out from under the bed.

Trying not to panic, I pulled Duffy aside for a little conference. "I know, I thought he'd get bored with it, too, but look at him! *Gleep, gleep.* What do you think Mrs. Varner's going to say when she comes home and hears that?"

Duffy shook his head. "I don't exactly know, Peter."

"She's going to say we put him up to it, that's what," I informed him. "She might even think it was part of that secret method you advertised in your flyer . . . if she ever reads it."

While we were talking, Andrew hopped out of the room and down the hall gleeping happily. Brian, shrieking his encouragement, trailed close behind.

"Hey, watch 'em," I shouted, ending our discussion fast. "Duffy! They're getting away!"

Duffy gripped his fingers tight around the handle of Joe's cage. "Hold on, Joe. We're *moving!*"

He bolted toward the door, swinging Joe's Tiny Traveler high in the air, and I sprinted after him, stumbling over my feet.

At the top of the stairs, I skidded to a stop. "Which way did they go?" I hollered at Duffy, who was already on the bottom step.

"Toward the kitchen," he yelped and Niagara Joe bokked. "I think they may be headed for the back door!"

"Great," I muttered. "Now we'll never catch 'em."

I knew for a fact the Varners had an unfenced yard—none of the yards on that side of the street were fenced—so the kids would be loose. Who could tell where they'd go? Or how fast!

"Duffy, is that back door locked? I'm worried."

He disappeared into the kitchen. "Hey, Andrew! Keep your hands off that hook!"

Andrew, when it wasn't convenient to be a frog, was a

pretty good squirrel. In no time flat, he'd shoved a high wooden stool to the door and unlocked it.

"Peter, there they go!"

Talk about fast moving kids! They streaked across the lawn like twin bolts of lightning, and when we finally caught up with them, they were next door, in the neighbor's garden.

"Oh, *no!*" I groaned. "Duffy, say it's only a bad dream!"

It wasn't.

Andrew was seated amidst the lilies in a shallow lily pond, and Brian was happily splashing water over his head. The neighbors, fortunately, were nowhere in sight.

"Guh-leep," Andrew gurgled, as the water trickled down his face.

"An-doo's a real *frog!*" Brian squealed. "Look!"

I did, and it was awful. Oh, the kids weren't in danger of drowning or anything, but I could see *Duffy Moon, Inc.* going under.

So could Duffy, because he just collapsed on a bench beside the pool and held his head in his hands.

"Well, I guess this queers it for us on babysitting jobs," he said, glumly. "I wonder what we did wrong?"

"Maybe your thought waves just work on people and they got sidetracked when Andrew turned into a frog."

I heard a woman's footsteps clattering across the patio and spun around.

"Are those my boys?" Mrs. Varner shrieked, picking up speed. "Andrew? Brian?"

I ran over and tried to explain. "It was like this . . ." I began, hoping she had a sense of humor.

Duffy finished. "He makes a neat frog, Mrs. Varner. I hope you can appreciate that."

She couldn't and lost no time telling us.

But she took a couple of dollars from her purse anyway. Quietly. With her lips tight together like they were stitched shut. Then she gathered up her boys and left us standing in a puddle of water with a couple of uprooted lily pads at our feet.

"I wish we'd had a chance to go back to the house," Duffy said later, after we'd put the pond back in order. "I wanted to tell her why the lower leaves were falling off her dieffenbachia."

Chapter 6

''HAVE YOU ever considered delivering papers?'' I asked Duffy the next day on our way home from paying off the printer. "A lot of businessmen got their start that way and today they're big tycoons."

"The newspaper said there aren't any openings right now and I can't wait. I want to make a name for myself this summer!"

"Well, I'm all for that, but I sure wish you'd find another way to do it. I got a threatening phone call last night from a kid who knew we did some babysitting yesterday."

Duffy stopped in his tracks. "Why didn't you tell me? What did he say?"

"He said we should buzz off. And when I reminded him that the job wasn't even one *Help Is Here* wanted, he said it didn't matter. They might want it next time, and it was the principle of the thing."

"Principle, my foot. They're just afraid of a little honest competition."

"I know, Duffy. Which is why they have no right to be mad. So far we haven't given them any competition."

Duffy kicked at a stone. "We will. We just haven't had the right calls yet. The kinds of jobs where I can really show off my secret method."

It was obvious he wasn't going to let our failure of the day before undermine his self-confidence. Or shake his faith that cosmic awareness would bring him everything he desired.

"It got Andrew out from under the bed, didn't it? So you see, Peter, we proved we were experts in that respect. Talking Andrew into playing frog was our mistake. A mistake that we just won't make again the next time we're called on to babysit."

"The next time?" I squawked, unable to believe my ears. "What makes you think there'll be a next time? By now, every mother in seven counties has heard what we did to Andrew. Or seen him. Ughh. I wonder how long he'll keep it up."

Not forever, because the following day we met up with

Mrs. Varner outside the supermarket and Andrew was there, a regular kid again.

My first thought was did he have any after effects, but none had shown up as far as I could see . . . not even a froggy smile.

"Mama," Andrew shouted, clapping his hands. "It's Doctor Small . . . and Peter!"

Mrs. Varner sighed. Then, in a voice a whole lot more friendly than she'd used on us before, she said, "You know, I really have to apologize for losing my temper the other day. You *were* doing your best, and the boys *are* unpredictable."

She glanced down at Andrew, who was tugging at her sleeve.

"Would you believe they liked the two of you better than any other babysitters?"

"No kidding?" Duffy asked, surprised.

"It's all they talk about," Mrs. Varner continued. "And they've been begging me to go out again so you'll come back."

I gulped hard.

"Will you? I need some time to myself and Mr. Varner's already put a better lock on the back door."

Mumbling something about having a partner, Duffy looked at me and I nodded. What could I say?

Like me, he probably figured we'd do better next time. At least we'd know what to expect, which was half the battle.

What I was afraid of was that Andrew and Brian would do us in before Boots McAfee. There certainly was a chance they would. And it made life risky. Too risky.

"Duffy, promise me something. We aren't going to specialize in babysitting jobs, are we? Because I don't think I could take it."

Duffy acted surprised. "Of course not, Peter. What we're after are the really difficult assignments. The jobs that are too tough for anyone else."

The next day I found out what he meant when we got the first call that was a direct response to our flyer.

"It was a Mrs. Charles who lives over on Wentworth near the library," Duffy said, as he put down the phone. "Her Great Dane rolled in some fish heads and needs a bath."

There was a sinking feeling in my stomach. "You mean Colonel? Duffy, I know that dog. He's as wild as they come. About a year ago, he knocked me flat when I walked by their house on my way to the library." I shuddered, remembering. "And he was just a pup then! Have you seen him lately?"

Duffy shook his head, but I could tell that my opinion

of Colonel wasn't going to change his mind.

"I'll take care of him," he said reassuringly. "I'll just picture him tame as a baby lamb in the bathtub and my powers of thought control will do the rest."

He closed his eyes to concentrate.

I tried to do the same, but the picture I conjured up was terrible to behold. It showed Colonel chasing us down the street in a flurry of soap suds with Mrs. Charles in the background screaming.

"Duffy, I don't think it'll work. Colonel's not the kind of dog who'll sit still for a bunch of thought waves. Suppose he leaps right out of your frequency?"

"He won't," Duffy replied with complete confidence. "Because I have an idea of my own that I think will prevent that. All I have to do is track down the proper equipment and you can help me do that right now."

"Equipment?"

He didn't explain. He just grabbed my arm and we sailed out the door past his Aunt Peggy, who was returning home with an armload of groceries, and down the stairs to the street below.

"So where are we going?" I demanded as we steered our bikes out into the traffic.

"To see a lady I know who grows her own herbs," Duffy

shouted over his shoulder. "I met her at the library once when we were both after the same book, and she invited me over to see her garden anytime I wanted to come."

He signaled for a right turn and we started up a hill. "I've (puff) gone over there a couple of times. And she's (puff) a real nice lady, Peter. You'll like her."

"I'm sure I will," I replied, pedalling hard to keep up with him. "But what's she got to do with Colonel?"

"You'll see," Duffy said mysteriously. "Herbs aren't grown just to cook with, Peter. Lots of people think they have (puff) supernatural powers!"

"Terrific," I gasped. "Because we're going to need that kind of help to get Colonel into a tub. He's as big as a Shetland pony, Duffy. You gotta see him to believe it."

There were worse jobs than babysitting, I realized sadly. And with Duffy in charge, we were going to try our hand at all of them.

Could he find a way to make cosmic awareness work for this assignment? I wondered.

I was still wondering when we reached the herb lady's house about ten minutes later.

"I sure hope she's home," I whispered, as Duffy rang the bell.

"She usually is," he said in his deep voice. "She isn't the

type to belong to a lot of clubs and stuff. She told me she'd rather stay home with her dog."

It was because she had a dog that we'd left Niagara Joe behind. He was a black faced Pug, as fat as a balloon in Macy's Christmas parade, and he met us at the door when the herb lady opened it.

"Mrs. Paxson, this is my friend Peter Finley," Duffy said politely.

"How very nice to meet you," Mrs. Paxson replied, showing us in. "This is Chang. We have visitors, my dear. Say hello to the nice boys."

Chang snorted and waddled around in circles, wagging his curly tail.

"Mrs. Paxson, I came to see you because I have a real problem."

"What, Duffy? Need some garden space to grow a few plants?"

"No, it's more complicated than that," Duffy replied, as we trailed behind Mrs. Paxson on her way to the kitchen.

I recognized the aroma of yeast dough in the air.

"I'm trying out my doughnut recipe for the Win-A-Fortune Cooking Contest," she explained, hurrying back to the stove. "It's original. Won't you boys try one of them? Let me know what you think, and then we can talk."

I ate the doughnut she handed me, but it was pretty greasy. And tough. Not at all like the doughnuts my father made, but, of course, I didn't say that. What I said was that they were very good.

Mrs. Paxson beamed. "Oh, I'm so glad you think so, Peter. Maybe that means that this year I'll win something. I enter every contest, you know, because it's always been my dream to be a famous cook and write a cookboook or a cooking column like Grace Gallagher."

I stopped with my doughnut in mid-air, but Duffy covered up my surprise with some fast talking. "Why not write a book about herbs, Mrs. Paxson? You know everything there is to know about them. In fact, that's why I came to see you."

"Oh?"

"Yes, I want you to tell me if there's any herb that will subdue a wild animal."

Mrs. Paxson's eyes opened wide. "Well, there's Aniseed, which was given to horses with toothaches in the seventeenth century. And there's Hare's Thistle, which was supposed to cure rabbits of a type of madness. But those are both domestic animals, aren't they?"

I nudged Duffy, who corrected himself. "I guess when you come right down to it, the animal we have in mind is domestic, too. Awfully frisky, though. A Great Dane."

"Oh, a dog?" Mrs. Paxson laughed. "You know, it's funny, but the herb artemisia—Silver Mound, some people call it—has a strange effect on some dogs. Met an Irish Wolfhound who was so enchanted with the smell that he ate an entire plant right to the ground." She looked down at her Pug. "Though Chang couldn't care less about it, isn't that peculiar?"

Duffy's eyebrows shot up. "You mean you have some artemisia in your garden now? Could we have a little slip of it?"

"My dear, I'll give you the whole plant, if you want it. Come outside. But remember, I can't guarantee it'll do what you want. Like I said, Chang isn't even remotely interested in it. Maybe your Great Dane'll feel the same way."

"I hope not," I said later on our way to the Charles'. In Duffy's hands were four or five stalks of the feathery grey plant. And Mrs. Paxson had promised we could come back for more anytime we needed it.

How Duffy planned to quiet Colonel with it was something I wanted to know.

"Oh, I'm not going to let him eat it, if that's what you're worried about. He could get sick. I'm going to tuck it inside my shirt. Like this. See?" He stuffed the stalks down the neck of his faded jersey.

"Echhh, Duffy! Isn't that kind of scratchy?"

"Not when I believe it isn't," he said, squirming. Then he made a face. "But, it has a sickening smell. Did you notice?"

I noticed. "Think that's why the dogs like it?"

Duffy shrugged. "Who can tell? We can't be sure of anything till we meet up with Colonel."

"Or he meets up with us," I muttered shakily. Which was an even stronger possibility.

When we arrived though, Colonel was tied to his doghouse and he smelled like a fishing boat just back with a catch.

"You can see why he needs a bath, boys," Mrs. Charles said from some distance away. "Do you think you can handle him? Two of the teenagers from *Help Is Here* tried and gave up on him yesterday. That's why I called you. Your flyer said no job was too tough."

Duffy straightened his shoulders and stood tall. Under any other circumstances, it would have helped his image, but dwarfed as he was next to Colonel, it only made him look ridiculous.

Mrs. Charles, fortunately, did not seem to notice. At least, she didn't say anything and I was thankful for that, because I could see that we were going to be in for it from another source. Three kids who were members of *Help Is*

Here had just pedaled by on their bikes, and they were turning around.

"Hey, shrimp," one of them shouted as soon as Mrs. Charles had gone inside. "What are you going to do with that racehorse? Ride him?"

Duffy pretended not to hear. "Be careful on the steps when you go in for more warm water, Peter. I spilled some coming out a second ago."

I rubbed my wet hands on my jeans. We were in the middle of the lawn filling up a big wash tub so we could bathe Colonel outside. He was too fishy to take down in the Charles' basement. And too big.

"See what I mean about him being wild, Duffy? Look at him lunging on the end of his chain over there! How're we ever going to get him into a bathtub?"

"We'll manage," Duffy replied. "If he'll calm down enough for me to practice my thought control. Think he can smell the herbs, Peter? They should be working."

I glanced over my shoulder at the kids across the street, who waved and chorused with a few catcalls. "I don't think he can smell anything but fish, Duffy. But that's not your fault," I added. "You didn't know how bad it would stink."

Duffy gave me this sad look. "D-don't give up now, Peter. Dr. Flamel says that's the worst thing you can do."

84

"Well, Dr. Flamel doesn't have Colonel to face! Or those kids across the street!"

I grunted and emptied the last bucket of water into the big galvanized tub. "And I had to complain about babysitting! Boy, I didn't know when I was well off."

Duffy closed his eyes for a minute and took a deep breath. Then he pulled down the brim of his floppy hat and tensed his muscles for the job ahead.

"I guess it's time to go get Colonel now," he croaked and his voice rose an octave. "You ready?"

"Ready as I'll ever be. But you stay awake," I hissed. "I'm not going to get flattened by that circus pony while you go into some kind of trance!"

Duffy motioned to me to be quiet, and as I stood there shaking, he approached the doghouse.

"Hi there, Colonel. Look into my eyes now. Want to come get a bath and get rid of that awful smell? *Whew!* Peter, he really stinks!"

"I know," I muttered and Colonel barked. Then he reared up on his hind legs, ready to play. I was ready to go home.

"Duffy, *wait!* Maybe you shouldn't unchain him just yet! He's wilder than he was a minute ago. He's going to get away from both of us!"

The kids across the street heard me shout and laughed. "Let the beast go!" they hooted. "We want to see him pulverize you!"

Duffy waited till Colonel was down on all fours and then unfastened the snap lock. "Come on, boy," he coaxed, trying to lead him by the collar. "Hey! Quit nuzzling me that way, will you? And watch those big feet of yours! You'll cripple me for life."

I won't say Colonel was a whole lot calmer, but all of a sudden, it was obvious he liked Duffy. And anywhere Duffy wanted to go was okay with him. In fact, he would gladly drag him there if Duffy didn't want to walk.

I held my breath. "Do you think the artem . . . that herb is working?" I asked, as we struggled to lift the front half of Colonel into the tub.

"It's got to be," Duffy replied hoarsely. "Look how interested he is in my shirt front. Hey! Cut it out, Colonel! You're going to drown me with that big tongue of yours."

I ignored the roars of laughter that came from the other side of the street, and sloshed a bucket of warm water over Colonel's back. "Got him, Duffy? I'm ready to pour on the suds."

Duffy was sitting on the ground in front of Colonel, holding his collar steady with both hands. "Pour away! I think I can hang on for . . . a . . . little . . . while . . .

at . . . least." He was trying in vain to get his face away from Colonel, who was washing every inch of it.

"Okay then, here goes," I said and dumped half a bottle of dog shampoo on Colonel's wet fur. "Whoops, sorry about that, Duffy. I can't wash Colonel's neck without getting your hands."

"Peterrrr . . . *help!*" The soap made Duffy's fingers slip from the collar just enough to give Colonel the advantage. The next thing I knew, Duffy was looking up at me from underneath Colonel, and still hanging on for dear life.

"You okay?"

"I g-guess so."

The *Help Is Here* gang cheered loudly.

"Then answer me this. How am I going to rinse Colonel with you down there where you'll get all wet?"

It was a knotty problem, but it didn't faze Duffy Moon, who was at one with the universe. He just closed his eyes, gave his orders, and I rinsed away—dumping bucket after bucket of water on Colonel—and Duffy.

"*Glubb,*" he choked once or twice, but I made sure he wasn't drowning. He was just having trouble catching his breath and avoiding Colonel, who was still trying to put his nose down Duffy's shirt front.

"We . . . did . . . it!" I shouted finally, and our audience reacted with surprised silence. "Still there, Duffy? Come on, easy now. Let's get this monster back on his chain!"

Duffy sputtered and emptied his hat which was full of water.

Mrs. Charles came out of the house. "You boys are absolutely marvelous," she gushed, as we tied up Colonel and

toweled him dry with some big bath towels. "But you're so *wet!* What happened? Did you get into the tub with him?"

Duffy screwed up his baby face. "Not exactly, but it came (sputter) close to that. I guess Colonel just wants to be friends. Don't you, boy?"

Colonel woofed and gave Duffy another lick.

The boys across the street jumped on their bikes and sped away. But not before they shot us a few dirty looks and shook their fists at us behind Mrs. Charles' back.

Chapter 7

"SO WE'VE cornered the market in dog washing," I said on our way home. "How long can we last doing that kind of work? Look at you, Duffy. You're leaving a trail of water behind you like you just stepped out of a swimming pool. What are you going to tell your Aunt Peggy? That you were hosed down by a fire truck?"

Duffy paused. "I could tell her the truth, I guess. But I'd rather go over to your place and run my clothes through your dryer. My aunt thinks I take on too much sometimes. She's like you. She doesn't realize that with cosmic awareness I can do anything."

I studied the puddle gathering around his feet. "Well, maybe you can do anything, but *I* can't. Any more jobs like the ones we've had and I'll be a hospital case! And I'm not even mentioning what condition I'll be in after Boots McAfee is through!"

"Boots McAfee, hah!" Duffy snorted. "I'm not afraid of him. The harder I work at my cosmic awareness, the tougher I feel."

"I know, Duffy. It's given you a lot of self-confidence. But that's *all* it's done. Everything else has happened because . . . you've *made* it happen. Like the way you built that rock wall, and hung on to Colonel when he got a whiff of your herbs!"

"You're just saying that to knock Dr. Flamel, Peter. I was a nobody before I sent for his course. And now I'm on my way to being *somebody* . . . with him to thank."

We didn't say any more. And for the next two blocks, the only sound I heard was the squoosh of water in Duffy's shoes.

A few days passed. Then one morning Duffy shook me and Dodger out of bed with the news that we'd just had another call. This one from a lady with a problem in her basement.

"Did she say what kind of a problem?" I yawned sleepily. Groggy as I was, I wasn't that groggy. After our encounters with the Varner kids and that horse Colonel, I was beginning to get a little wary.

Duffy picked up my jeans from the floor and threw them at me. "She didn't go into any detail on the phone, but she sounded pretty rattled. We're supposed to drop by as soon as we can and talk to her about it."

Her name was Mrs. Toby and I don't think she was much older than Duffy's Aunt Peggy, but it was hard to tell from the way she looked. Her blond hair was sticking out every which way and she had dark circles under her eyes the way people do when they don't get enough sleep.

For all we knew, she'd been trying to sleep when we came. She still had on a flowered housecoat and a pair of terrycloth bedroom slippers.

"Are you boys from *Duffy Moon, Inc.?*" She pushed at her hair.

Duffy nodded.

"Well, I called you because of what you said in your flyer. You remember . . . that no job's too tough?"

I swallowed hard and she motioned to us to come inside so she could get back to a mug of black coffee on the kitchen table.

"I have (sniff) a terrible problem that no one seems to

be able to solve. Not even the police!"

Duffy's eyes opened wide.

"You see," Mrs. Toby began in a very shaky, little girl voice. "There's this strange noise in my basement—kind of off and on all night—and I just know there's *something down there!*"

"Something alive?" I gasped.

She snuffled back a tear. "Yes, and you can't imagine how frightened I am. I'm all alone here. My husband's away on business."

Duffy scratched his head. "What about the neighbors?"

"You mean did I call them?" Mrs. Toby asked. "Of course. The very first night. But, t-they couldn't find anything! Neither could the police! And now (sniff), they all say it must be my . . . i-imagination!"

"Imagination?" Duffy exploded. "How could it be that? After all you heard the noise. . . ."

"Yeah," I agreed and Mrs. Toby started to cry.

"It's because I'm all alone. The police say a lot of women get scared and think they hear something when their husbands are away. But I tell you, I'm not imagining this. How can a person imagine the sound of a dozen garden stakes clattering to the floor . . . when there they are?"

I stood up and tried to fight off the weakness that had suddenly spread over my whole body.

"You f-found garden stakes on the floor?" Duffy croaked.

"Early this morning. That's why I called you boys. I want you to help me. No one else will."

"Duffy, I wish you'd give me a chance to talk before you take on these jobs!" We were sitting on Mrs. Toby's back steps having a conference. "This one gives me goose pimples clear down to my toes."

"It makes me a little jittery, too," Duffy admitted. "But that'll pass when I put my cosmic awareness to work. Quiet, now. I have to concentrate. I have to picture us down in Mrs. Toby's basement finding her noise."

I thought of what a nice day it would be for playing street hockey and took a deep breath. "You picture us down in Mrs. Toby's basement. I'd rather be home playing hockey . . . or walking Dodger."

"That's it!" Duffy yelled, his voice cracking. "We go back to your house and get Dodger! He's a terror! And if there's anything . . . anything at all down in that basement, he'll root it out."

It occurred to me that the *anything* might be *someone*,

but I put it straight out of my mind. Dodger was our only chance. We told Mrs. Toby we were going to deputize him and send him down ahead of us as a kind of scout.

"That's fine," she said, dabbing at her eyes with a clean tissue. "A good watch dog is a valuable animal to have. I wish I had one myself."

"I sure hope whatever Dodger finds is something we can . . . handle," I said after we'd run home and taken him from his toys. "A job like this isn't quite the same as taking care of kids, you know."

"No, but it's a challenge," Duffy said, squaring his shoulders.

"A challenge?" We stopped to let Dodger sniff at a tree. "Duffy, I don't think you're getting my point. I'm worried about our safety! Suppose Dodger flushes out a dangerous criminal. Or . . . something worse."

"Like a hideous fungus that devours people alive?" We'd just seen one of those on an afternoon horror film. "Peter, quit trying to scare me. You know yourself we promised Mrs. Toby we'd find her noise."

"I know, but does the noise know it? Duffy, Dodger's never done anything like this before . . . on a professional basis. He just plays watchdog around our house."

"But I thought you told me that Yorkies were once used in Scotland to catch rats and snakes."

"Yes, but Yorkies were bred bigger then. They weren't the tiny teacups they are today."

"Dodger's no tiny teacup," Duffy said.

"True," I replied, studying the silky mop at my feet. "But sometimes he thinks I want him to be. So he's never sure. It's like he's torn between being a tiger and a teacup, you know what I mean?"

Mrs. Toby was surprised that Dodger wasn't a German Shepherd. "I thought, from the way you described him, that . . ."

"He was huge?"

"Well, yes-s-s."

Poor Dodger. Now someone was saying he was too small.

Duffy settled things with a wave of his hand. "Don't worry, Mrs. Toby. Just leave the problem to us. We're going down into your basement now and when we come back up, all your fears will be a thing of the past."

I figured that last was a quote from Dr. Flamel, because it sure wasn't something a kid would say. "All your fears will be a thing of the past, Mrs. Toby," I mimicked as we tiptoed down the basement stairs. "What kind of talk is that, Duffy? How can you be so sure we're going to find whatever's down here? The police couldn't!"

Duffy silenced me with a look. Then he said, "Come on, Peter. Dodger's already at the foot of the steps. And he's sniffing around like he's on the trail of something. What a tiger!"

"Atta way to go, Dodger," I whispered, ashamed suddenly that I had ever doubted him. "He just scooted through that open door, Duffy. Let's follow him!"

The Tobys' basement was broken up into rooms, the way the basements in most old houses are. And it was dark and musty smelling.

Duffy sneezed.

"I'll bet you anything they take in a little water down here," I murmured, sniffing the air. "Sure is a dungeon, huh? Like something out of a horror movie."

Duffy closed his eyes and took a deep breath. "I . . . picture . . . us . . . getting . . . out . . . of . . . here . . . alive. And finding Mrs. Toby's noise at the same time!"

"Good show," I whispered. "Now open those blinkers and let's go. Dodger's hot on a scent!"

Wooff! he barked, not sure yet what he was barking at.

There was a rattle, then a clatter from a corner near the wash tubs.

Rowr-rr-row! Dodger growled, the snarl coming from

low in his throat. He took off in the direction of the rattle.

"I . . . uh, thought Mrs. Toby said she only heard the noises at night," I said nervously.

"She did. Do you see anything?"

"No, but whatever made that sound must be over there."

Rowruff! Dodger ducked between the wall and a couple of old bushel baskets. *Woof!* he backed out again, his eyes bright.

"Go get 'em, tiger!" I shouted encouragingly. "Come on, Duffy. Let's see what he's got cornered."

It couldn't be anything too big.

Dodger growled and went in head first. "Watch out," I warned, but it was too late. The thing fought back. And one of the bushel baskets clattered to the floor.

Dodger yelped and retreated, pawing his nose.

I bounded forward. "I'm going in there, Duffy."

At first, when I peered into the darkness, I couldn't see anything. Then I made out a small, rounded form and finally—when my eyes adjusted themselves—I spotted a toad. A very frightened one, staring out at me through folds of fat.

"What'd you find?" Duffy asked, leaning over my shoulder. "Hey, is that a toad?"

Mrs. Toby came to the stairs and shouted down. "What's happening? Are you kids okay?"

Dodger was barking furiously.

"Everything's fine, Mrs. Toby," Duffy yelled and clapped me on the shoulder.

"It's just a toad! He must have gotten down here by mistake in some garden things . . . or maybe through one of your basement windows. Do you ever leave any of them open?"

"Well, sometimes," Mrs. Toby said, venturing down a few steps. "But only when my husband's home." She made a face. "You mean it's actually a live toad? Ughh," she said, as I held it up with its fat oozing through my fingers. "Kill it!"

Duffy was horrified. "Mrs. Toby! You can't want that! Toads are valuable creatures. They'll stay in your garden and eat thousands of insects every summer if you give them a chance. Some people even go out looking for toads, just for that purpose! Besides," he added, surprising even me, "it's considered lucky if a toad enters your house. Didn't you know that?"

Mrs. Toby shook her head. "No, and I didn't know all that stuff about toads being good in the garden, either. You must read a lot, huh?"

"Duffy's a member of the American Begonia Society," I informed her. "And a real plant expert, both indoors and out."

"Well, that's good news," she said, sitting down on the step. "Because I'm a complete blank when it comes to gardening. We just moved into this house a few months ago and I've got plants coming up out there I've never even seen before. Think you could take a look at them? I'll pay you. As a matter of fact, you and Peter can take over the whole garden. My husband told me to hire someone. I plan to spend most of the summer inside, redecorating the house."

Duffy was struck speechless. Then, when he finally did manage a reply, his voice rose a whole octave. "We . . . we . . ."

"We'll do it," I finished for him, amazed at how we had gone from strange sounds in the cellar to garden care.

"We sure will, Mrs. Toby. And thanks. I never thought of hiring myself out as a plant expert. I've always just kind of looked on it as fun."

It was strange, but I had a hunch that Duffy had just stumbled onto the first job that was tailor-made for him. And with it was going to come that big name he wanted for himself. How could he miss?

After all, taking care of people's plants was something Duffy could do better than anyone else.

And it wasn't even like *work* to him. Next to Niagara Joe, it was his true love.

Chapter 8

AS YOU might expect, though, Duffy said cosmic awareness was responsible for the whole thing. He was still a nothing without it, and he wasn't going to let a skeptic like me convince him otherwise.

My own opinion was that Duffy was a genius, and that sending Dodger down after that toad was about the smartest thing he'd ever done. Business-wise, I mean. Because from then on, we got calls almost every day. Not from people with rattlings in their basements, but from people who'd heard from Mrs. Toby about Duffy and his remarkable way with plants.

"That's the third phone call you've had today," Aunt Peggy said, just hanging up the receiver as we walked in the door. "From a Mrs. Smith wondering if you can take a look at her marigolds. Something's eating them—stripping them bare, as a matter of fact—and the spray she got from the hardware store hasn't helped a bit."

"Think we can fit her in after we do Mrs. Varner's roses?" I asked Duffy. "There should be enough time. The kids understand now why we can't stay and play with them."

Captain Smiles, who was still at home, handed me the address. "Duffy tells me you're the one who schedules all these jobs. That what you do best, Peter?"

"It's what I like a whole lot," I replied, opening my spiral notebook. "I also keep our accounts. See? Every cent we've earned is listed right here."

Captain Smiles whistled softly. "Not bad."

He pointed to some figures. "These your rates?"

"Yes, sir," I said. "Six dollars a week to take care of a lawn and garden while the owners are away on vacation. One dollar a week extra, if Duffy has to look after the house-plants. Twenty-five cents apiece to repot plants if the owner provides the pot, and fifty cents plus expenses if we have to get the pot ourselves."

"And this item you call a consultation?"

"Seventy-five cents, Ralph," Aunt Peggy said proudly.

"The boys have to charge something to make a house call, you know."

"That's right, Captain . . . er, Mr. Randall," I agreed. "A lot of people just want to be told what they're doing wrong. Or what it is that's eating their plants."

"The clerks at the hardware store aren't gardening experts," Aunt Peggy pointed out. "And even if they were, they wouldn't come out and look at a plant. The boys' service is more personal."

"I never make a diagnosis over the phone," Duffy announced solemnly.

Captain Smiles scratched his head. "Well, I'll be darned. That there's even a call for this sort of thing is hard to believe!" He stood back and measured Duffy with his eyes. "Now, hiring a kid to mow a lawn, I can understand. But to doctor plants?"

"Wonderful, isn't it?" Aunt Peggy said, putting her arm around Duffy. "I told you that he had a gift. That it was more than just a green thumb!"

Duffy blushed. He was embarrassed, I guess, by all the attention and went to his room to find Niagara Joe.

I followed, with the tray of sandwiches Aunt Peggy had made for our lunch and two glasses of milk.

There was something about our success that was worrying me and it wasn't how we were going to fit in Mrs. Smith's marigolds.

"It's more like what we're going to do about *Help Is Here*," I said, sitting down on the floor. "We're headed for a showdown, Duffy. And if I read my cards right, it'll be within a week, when Boots McAfee comes back from vacation!"

"I don't see how you can be so sure of that," Duffy replied, as he and Joe joined me on the rug. "We haven't been bothered by the *Help Is Here* gang since the day we bathed Colonel!"

He bit into a sandwich. "Go ahead, say it's because we're sneaky and they haven't caught us. But I tell you, it's because they've given up! They've seen how powerful someone with cosmic awareness can be, and they've just knuckled under."

"They've done nothing of the kind, Duffy," I said angrily, then lowered my voice so his aunt and uncle wouldn't hear us. "It's just that you're so sure you're superkid that the facts don't mean a thing to you!"

Duffy put down his sandwich. "What facts?"

"Facts like this. *Duffy Moon, Inc.* has definitely cut into some of the *Help Is Here* business. Oh, I know, we've only taken away the jobs we're best at, but that doesn't mean anything to them. They're mad, Duffy, and eventually it'll turn into a real fight between us and them. Maybe all twenty-five of them!"

I leaned back on my hands, rattled just from talking about it. But had I made an impression on Duffy? Or even Niagara Joe?

Joe squawked.

Duffy just went on eating his sandwich. "So what if you're right?" he said in a cocky voice. "I don't care what they think. I told you before, there are enough jobs in this area for two outfits. Besides, I have cosmic awareness on my side and as long as I do, I'm completely protected by my shield of invulnerability!"

"That's a bunch of baloney!" I hissed, as loudly as I dared. "You believe in that . . . garbage when what you should be doing is digging a bomb shelter and hiding out in it! Who do you think kept you from getting pulverized that day we were passing out flyers?" I demanded, and Niagara Joe bokked me a good one. "Not Dr. Flamel! *Me,* Peter Finley. And my hockey stick!"

"Not so," Duffy said, taking apart the rest of his sandwich and rearranging the lettuce. "You just think it was you because you're a skeptic and Dr. Flamel said . . ."

"Wait, don't tell me. Dr. Flamel said that skeptics like me should be ignored, right?"

Duffy shrugged. "You're the one who said it."

I jumped up. "Listen, Duffy. You can take your whole business and . . . drop it in the sea! I don't want any part of it. Or you. Or Dr. Flamel! I'm trying to tell you the truth, you fruitcake! And if you're going to take the word of that gyp artist over mine, you just let *him* protect you next time you meet up with trouble!"

I threw down my napkin and beat it out of there fast. I sure didn't want Duffy to see me crying. And dumb as it was, I felt kind of close to it at that moment.

Why I went into business with Duffy in the first place was more than I could understand. I knew all along it was going to get us into trouble. And now it had broken up our friendship besides. A double disaster.

"Pe-ter!" I heard Duffy call from the stairs as I reached the ground floor of the apartment building. "Pe-ter! Come back!"

I stumbled to the door.

"You're . . . still . . . my . . . partner!"

"I'm not anyone's partner anymore," I told my dad when I got back home. Dodger had jumped up into my lap and was licking my face. "I just wanted Duffy to know the truth. Before we have to . . ."

"What?" he asked.

"To explain everything t-to his Aunt Peggy and Captain Smiles."

I didn't dare tell my dad that *Help Is Here* was after us. He might call the police or something. And it was a problem we would have to face ourselves. Separately. The news that I was no longer Duffy's partner wasn't going to impress the kids at *Help Is Here*. I'd been with him for too long. And when Boots McAfee came back from his vacation, I was sure he'd get me along with Duffy. In separate alleys.

"Ughh. Dodger, you're the only one left I can talk to," I moaned and lugged him out to the porch where we sat on the front steps.

Dodger struggled out of my grasp and ran after his rubber duck.

"Not now," I said, as he pushed it at me for a game of fetch. "Can't you see I'm a doomed man? I need time to think."

Duffy called that night, but I'd already gone to bed. Then on Saturday, my dad and I went down to the Jersey shore for three days, so I didn't see Duffy again until late Monday night when he came to the house.

"I don't want to talk to him," I told my dad, who'd answered the door.

"What kind of nonsense is that?" he demanded. "Duffy's your best friend. Besides, he and Joe look kind of shaken up. You better get downstairs and find out what's the matter!"

I dropped the TV magazine I'd been studying and jumped to my feet.

"Duffy? You still there?" I called out as I sailed down the steps.

Dodger was already in the hall, smothering him with kisses.

Duffy leaned against the wall. "Peter," he gasped like he'd been running for blocks. "I j-just met up with twelve *Help Is Here* kids down by the l-library." His floppy hat was gone, his hair was a mess, and there was a big three-cornered tear in his Uncle Ralph's football jersey.

"Are you hurt?" I asked, blaming myself for not being there with him. "What happened?"

"It was like you said, they're really after us. Tonight . . . they said tonight was just a sampling!" He rubbed at a place on his arm. "Tomorrow when Boots McAfee gets back they're going to finish the job!"

I got weak in the knees just thinking about it.

Dodger barked.

"I tried my cosmic awareness, but it didn't seem to

work," Duffy said miserably. "They had me and Joe surrounded, Peter, and I guess I was so scared they'd hurt Joe that I just couldn't concentrate. I couldn't even think, much less picture them running from me! What do you think'll happen now? How am I ever going to defeat Boots McAfee if I can't even get the best of his gang?"

"I don't know, Duffy," I groaned. "But when the time comes, he'll have to fight both of us, because I'm your partner again."

I dabbed at a scratch over his eye with the corner of my pajama. We might as well go down the tubes together. It'd be over quicker that way and neither of us would have a long wait.

Chapter 9

THAT NIGHT Duffy stayed at our house because he was too scared to walk home. It was a simple matter to clear it with his Aunt Peggy, and my dad was so used to Duffy sleeping over that he never suspected the real reason. Having him around, though, meant we did have to keep our voices down while we worked out a plan.

"What time of day is Boots expected home?" I asked Duffy in the kitchen where the four of us, Niagara Joe and Dodger included, had gone for a snack.

Neither of us were particularly hungry, but I took out the frypan anyway to make a couple of reversible eggs. Dodger had his feet up against the stove waiting and Niagara Joe was walking around in circles on the kitchen table.

I repeated the question.

"Oh, from vacation?" replied Duffy, who'd been deep in thought. "I don't know exactly, but I have a feeling that his gang will be right there waiting to tell Boots about us when his family pulls in the driveway."

I shuddered and cracked the first egg into the pan.

"Peter? It really bothers me that I couldn't get my cosmic awareness working for me tonight. What do you suppose is *wrong*?"

"Duffy, I *told* you . . ."

"No, wait. I think we should go in and see Dr. Flamel about it. Ask him in person."

The second egg broke in my hand.

"You mean like make an appointment? And go clear into the city?"

Niagara Joe bokked.

"Maybe we wouldn't need an appointment," Duffy said. "Besides, I don't have his phone number. I thought we could just find his address on a map and then take the train to the nearest stop."

I yanked the frypan off the burner and turned to face Duffy, potholder in hand. "What would we tell your Aunt Peggy? And my dad?"

Duffy shrugged. "I don't know. That we were only going as far as Glencote, maybe. The Bauder Arboretum is there. I've spent the whole afternoon wandering through it. My aunt wouldn't give it a second thought if I wanted to go again."

Dodger scratched at the stove for the eggs.

"But, Duffy . . ."

"Come on, Peter. It's really important that I see him. He'll want to know if his theories suddenly don't work anymore. And maybe he'll be able to explain why, straighten things out so I'll have my full powers back again . . . in time for Boots McAfee!"

"What makes you think Dr. Flamel will even talk to you?" I scoffed, slamming the pan back on the stove. "He already has your $7.98. Suppose he wants more money just to let you in the door?"

Duffy emptied his pockets and frowned. "Well, he'd better not. Because all I have with me is what I collected from jobs this afternoon. Enough for train fare and about forty cents extra, if we want a soda."

Niagara Joe picked up a dollar bill and dropped it over the edge of the table.

"Well?" Duffy said, retrieving it. "Will you go, Peter? Or do I have to go alone?"

He looked at me in such an earnest way that I sighed with exasperation. "Okay, okay," I said, crossing the kitchen to the refrigerator for another egg. "I'll go, but only so you can see for yourself what a crook Dr. Flamel is. Then we'll come back and defend ourselves the Finley way . . . with a couple of hockey sticks!"

"Bok," shrieked Niagara Joe.

Like Duffy said, we had no trouble convincing his aunt and my dad that we were taking the train into the Bauder Arboretum. Neither of them had the time to drive us, so they were glad we'd suggested going alone.

The only hitch in the plan came when my dad made me leave Dodger behind. Small as he was, we were counting on him to protect us, because—according to the map—Dr. Flamel lived in a pretty rough neighborhood. But my dad didn't know that. He just said, "You can't smuggle a dog into the arboretum, Peter, even if you were able to get him past the conductor on the train. Where would you hide him? He's too big for your pocket!"

"I thought I'd put him in a shopping bag," I said lamely. "Along with my old gray sweater. He likes that sweater. It'll keep him quiet."

My dad put Dodger back in his basket. "He's staying home."

"So we can't take Dodger," Duffy said later as we

boarded the train. "It'll be all right, Peter. We'll just keep our eyes open and get our business over as quickly as we can."

"Okay, because I know for a fact there are a lot of street gangs down there, and if we run into one of them, there won't be enough left of us for *Help Is Here*."

"Very funny," Duffy said, but he didn't laugh.

I found two seats and took the one by the window. In a second or two, the engineer blew the whistle and the train lurched forward on its way to the city. It was hot in our car, and after a while, the rhythmic jerk of the train from side to side made me sleepy.

"Uh-huh? What did you say?" I asked Duffy, when I opened my eyes and caught him nudging me.

"I said we're getting close to our stop, Peter. Look out the window. Somewhere down there is Dr. Flamel . . . with the answer to all our problems."

I doubted that, but I looked out of the window anyway. The patches of woods and the rolling golf courses were far behind. Now we saw only the backs of tenements and tree-less streets of stores and warehouses.

On the map in front of us, Duffy'd made an X where Dr. Flamel was.

"This is it!" he said, jumping up as the train squeaked

to a dusty standstill. "Let's go, Peter. Quick! Before we start moving again."

There was no danger. The conductor saw us coming. "Hey! Take it ea-sy, boys," he said in a friendly way. "Where you headed for . . . a fire?"

We bypassed some interesting looking graffiti on the station wall and sprinted down a flight of wooden steps.

"Over here," Duffy said, his map in hand. "See? Euclid Avenue. If we cross the street where that sign shop is, we can follow it to the next intersection. Dr. Flamel's place should be just a half a block down from that. On a little side street."

I brushed the sweat from my forehead. "Okay, Duffy. I hope you know what you're doing. You watch the map and I'll keep looking back toward the station so we can find it again when we want it."

There is something about being in a strange neighborhood that is kind of scary. A person doesn't know what's around the next corner, for one thing, and if you're on foot, you get the feeling that people are staring at you from every window and doorway.

"Duffy, maybe we should stop for a cold soda. Now, before we go any further. There's a sign over there on that grocery store."

116

Duffy yanked at my sleeve. "No, I'm in a hurry to find Dr. Flamel, Peter. Don't you understand? If my cosmic awareness is gone, everything'll go back to the way it was. I have to find out what's *wrong!*"

"Duffy . . ." There was no use arguing with him. He just trudged on ahead of me, his jaw set, and I followed.

Talk about scary neighborhoods. Things got even creepier when we turned down the little side street where Dr. Flamel was supposed to live and found it deserted. Really deserted.

The windows on most of the stores and the rowhouses opposite them were boarded up, and—except for us—the only living thing on the sidewalk was a stray cat, climbing into a garbage can.

I took a deep breath.

"Duffy, I h-hate to tell you t-this, but I think we're the only human beings on this block."

"You're mistaken," Duffy replied, without a backward glance.

I persisted. "Maybe we should go back home. You can write Dr. Flamel a letter. I'll even help you."

Duffy turned around and glared. "And how are we going to do that if Boots puts us in traction?" He plunged on ahead.

"But, I d-don't think Dr. Flamel is even here anymore, Duffy. Do you see any house numbers? I don't see a single one."

Something clattered on the sidewalk behind us, but when I wheeled around it was just the lid of the cat's garbage can vibrating on the cement.

"Thirty-two forty-four. Here it is, Peter!" Duffy whooped and pointed triumphantly to some metal letters tacked over a rundown shop. "But . . . but it doesn't say Felicity Sales anyplace! And it looks like it's closed!"

I had a sinking feeling that he was right. There was a heavy padlock through the bolt on the front door and the shades were drawn on the windows.

Chapter 10

"HEY!" Duffy shouted, rattling the door-knob. "Anyone in there? Open up!"

He beat on the door furiously, while I peeked under the window shade at the darkness inside.

"Face it, Duffy," I said after about five minutes. "There's no one here."

Duffy wouldn't give up. "Wait, let me try just once more." He hammered on the door with both fists. "Dr. Flamel! It's Duffy Moon. *Open up!*"

Presently, there was the sound of a window scraping open from across the street, and when we turned around, we saw an old guy peering at us from one of the rowhouses.

"What do you want?" he growled angrily. "Can't you

see the place is closed up? No one's there."

Duffy shaded his eyes from the sun that glared down on the cement. "I'm looking for Dr. Flamel. Dr. Louis B. Flamel." He crossed the street so he could see a little better. "Hey, is that you?"

The old man was startled.

"It is you, isn't it?" Duffy croaked, motioning for me to come. "I almost didn't recognize you. You've cut off your beard."

"What do you want?" Dr. Flamel asked nervously, and looked up and down the street.

"I want to talk to you," Duffy said, dragging me up the steps. "Please, Dr. Flamel. Come around to the door."

Dr. Flamel disappeared behind the curtains and we stood on the steps of his house for a long time.

"Duffy, I don't think we should. . . ."

The door creaked open.

"Well?" Dr. Flamel boomed and scowled down at us both. "Who are you?" There was a toothpick sticking out of his mouth and it jumped up and down when he spoke.

"I'm D-Duffy Moon, sir," Duffy said, awestruck. "One of your students. And this is my friend, Peter Finley."

Dr. Flamel scratched his head. "One of my students?"

"Yes sir. In cosmic awareness. You remember. I sent for your home study course the first week in June.

"You see," he rattled on as Dr. Flamel stared at him in absolute astonishment. "I've run into this problem. But it's just a minor one, I'm sure. Until yesterday, everything worked out just as you said it would. I have my own business, I've made a name for myself, and Peter and I are getting rich."

The toothpick nearly fell out of Dr. Flamel's mouth when Duffy said the word rich.

"Whoaa. Hold it, boy. You'll have to speak more slowly. Why don't you and . . . uh, Peter, step into my study. Then we can sit down—out of this blinding sun—and you can tell me your whole story."

He turned and Duffy started to follow him.

"Duffy, let's go," I begged, but it was no use. I took one last look at the deserted street and trailed after Duffy into Dr. Flamel's study.

My first impression was that the old man was getting ready to move. There were five or six stacks of books piled next to an empty box on the floor, an open trunk standing in the dining room archway and a half-eaten sandwich on top of a typewriter case.

"You'll have to excuse the appearance of my quarters right now," Dr. Flamel said, noticing my expression. "I'm lecturing at a university in Berlin next week and I have to get my notes packed so I can leave tonight."

He pulled out a white handkerchief and slapped at a spot on a fat, broken down sofa. I didn't sit down, but Duffy did, causing a cloud of dust to billow up.

"Ahh," Dr. Flamel said to Duffy. "Let me look at you. One of my students, are you? And you say you've mastered cosmic awareness, just as it's described in my book?"

Duffy nodded. And then he told Dr. Flamel everything that had happened, right down to the moment his cosmic energy particles failed him in front of the library.

"Ummmm," Dr. Flamel said and the toothpick stopped moving for almost a full minute. "That's a very interesting story, my boy. You did all that? Just from the instructions in my book?" He seemed surprised, as if he hardly dared believe it himself. "I must write down excerpts of your story for my notes," he murmured, pulling out a pocket tablet. "Particularly the details of your work with herbs. Some of my other students will benefit from your experiences. Why, I, myself. . . ."

"Dr. Flamel?" I interrupted, not about to let him pick Duffy's brain for new ideas. "Duffy and I have to get back home. Do you think you could explain why his cosmic awareness fizzled out on him yesterday? He's really counting on you to tell him," I added innocently. "So how about it?"

It bugged me that he was still trying to con Duffy into believing that he was a genuine scientist. And it double bugged me that Duffy was swallowing it. He never once noticed all the things that were fishy about the man. Like the fact that the nameplate on his trunk said John Davenport and not Dr. Flamel. And that one of the books waiting to be packed was on how to be a success as a door-to-door salesman.

"Duffy," I hissed. "Take a look around you."

Dr. Flamel caught me studying a carton of vegetable slicers and pushed them out of the way with his foot.

"Well, now. Let's get down to the . . . difficulty you describe." He stroked his nonexistent beard. "My professional opinion is that you were just temporarily unable to concentrate. And, of course, if you cannot visualize the desired picture in your mind, the cosmic energy particles lose their ability to fuse together. They break up into nothingness in the auric atmosphere."

I groaned. Leave it to Dr. Flamel to have an explanation for everything.

Moving aside a striped suitcase that was tied shut with twine, the man walked over to his trunk and began digging through it. "Stand back now," he snapped, as I peered over his shoulder. "It may take me a minute to find what I'm looking for, and I don't need your help."

He yanked open a drawer. "Somewhere I have a powerful charm that I know will give Duffy the boost he needs. It's made of aromatic Sraktya wood—from Madagascar—and it's guaranteed to bestow on its possessor the courage of a tiger and the strength of a bull!"

He pulled out a key chain with a varnished wooden bear hanging from it, and I remembered having seen something like it on a carnival midway.

"Hey, wait a minute," I protested.

"Oops, wrong charm," Dr. Flamel said, putting it back. "Here's the right one. Impressive-looking, huh? No two are exactly alike, you know. They're hand carved from a tree the natives call the Tree of Invulnerability."

As Duffy walked toward us, his eyes wide, Dr. Flamel dangled this hunk of wood in front on him on a leather thong.

"It'll give you the confidence you need to lick your oppressors," he said persuasively and turned his back on me. "What's more, it'll only cost you $4.98 . . . cash on the line."

Duffy turned white. "But that's too much!"

"Too much? Why, my boy, that's a bargain! I've already subtracted the shipping charges because you're buying direct."

"But . . ."

I was furious. The time had come to step in and give Duffy a little free help. "Look, Dr. Flamel," I said testily. "We only have forty cents between us . . . and return trip train tickets. So I guess Duffy can't buy your magic charm, after all. Besides," I added, "I don't believe it's everything you say it is anyway. Any more than I believe in your *phony book!*"

"Peter!" Duffy gasped. "Please!"

Dr. Flamel's toothpick jiggled up and down as if it were keeping time to an Irish jig. "Aha! Do I detect a skeptic in our midst?" He coughed nervously. "Well, I tell you what I'll do, but only because I've taken a personal interest in your case, Duffy. I'm going to give you this charm for forty cents. As a kind of reward for being one of my finest students."

"Some reward," I muttered and they both turned to glare at me.

It looked as though Duffy would be counting on cosmic awareness for at least one more fight. And when that was over, well, I didn't know what would happen. If he lost all his confidence, he'd be back thinking he was a nobody again. With nothing on his mind but the fact that he was small.

Chapter 11

"I DON'T know where you get off giving me the silent treatment," Duffy said when we were back on the train headed home. "It's my money. I can spend it any way I want!"

My eyes were riveted on the clusters of houses flashing by, and I kept them there, my back turned to Duffy.

"I know you can, but it's dumb, that's all. Anyone with half a brain could see for himself that Dr. Flamel is a big gyp artist. That open trunk, that pile of salesman books . . . he was getting ready to move on, Duffy! To some other place where he'll try a different scheme!"

Duffy was incensed. "How can you say that? He told us himself he was packing to leave for Europe and a lecture tour."

"With a book on how to be a door-to-door salesman and a carton of vegetable slicers? Come on, Duffy. Face the facts."

He grew silent. Then, in a voice that betrayed his first real doubt, he faltered, "I . . . am . . . facing . . . facts. The truth is that I was a nobody until I took Dr. Flamel's course in cosmic awareness. Everyone was always picking on me. I couldn't do anything I could be proud of. Why even my Uncle Ralph was embarrassed to have me around!"

"No, he wasn't," I protested, but not very convincingly.

"Yes, he was," Duffy insisted. "But now all that's changed. I'm president of my own company, Peter . . . and you're my partner. And when we go back to school in the fall and they want to know how we did it, I'll say it's because I've mastered cosmic awareness—the secret of the universe!"

"Then it's your own special kind. Because you could have done all that without Dr. Flamel's brand of cosmic power. All you needed was a little self-confidence and when you got that you made things happen on your own!"

Duffy's worst fear surfaced. "But that would mean I've just been fooling myself and down deep I'm still a shrimp who can't stand up to anyone."

"Well, you can't stand up to a gang like *Help Is Here* with the idea that you're indestructible! No one can be everything they want to be, Duffy. You gotta pick what you're good at and then work to make yourself the best."

I thought of all the people I knew and how none of them were satisfied. My dad, who had it in him to write a great cookbook, was struggling with a novel. Mrs. Paxson wanted to be a cook, but instead was a herb lady. Dodger wanted to be small. Duffy wanted to be big. It was ridiculous.

And depressing.

It was so depressing that I decided I didn't want to be *anything*. Just alive the next morning after we faced Boots McAfee.

Duffy sat still as a stone fingering his charm. He realized the truth in what I'd said—it was in his eyes—but he just couldn't accept it. It meant facing up to the certainty that we were going to be creamed the minute we got home.

Unless, I reasoned, we could defend ourselves with our hockey sticks or outsmart Boots's gang in some way. To me, neither seemed like a good possibility, but they were worth trying.

"Duffy, put the charm away and help me think of a plan," I begged when we finally reached our stop.

It was near suppertime and the station platform was crowded with commuters coming home from work.

"If Boots isn't waiting for us on my porch," I said, "maybe we'll have time to lay a trap for him. You know, scare the pants off him, and humiliate him so much in front of his gang that he won't come around anymore."

"That'd never work," Duffy said miserably.

"Well, it might. And as far as ideas go, it makes a lot more sense than a hunk of Sraktya wood and you standing around clutching it!"

Duffy winced. "You talk like it's worthless. Maybe it isn't. You haven't even given it a chance."

"It is worthless," I yelled. "And you're going to get hurt believing in it, Duffy. Because for the last time, magic is just for games. And for gyp artists like Dr. Flamel to sucker people out of their money."

When I warned Duffy he'd get hurt, I was thinking it would be by Boots McAfee. But even that would have been easier for him than what did happen.

"Hey, kids!" my dad shouted as we shuffled in the door. "The next time you take a day off, post it on a billboard, will you? Your Aunt Peggy and I have been taking phone calls all day, but nobody wants to take our word for it that you'll be on the job tomorrow."

I reached down to pet Dodger and Duffy rushed into the kitchen where he'd left Joe.

We hadn't had any real appointments, but that wasn't what was worrying me. "Did anyone named Boots McAfee call?" I asked nervously. "We were expecting him to . . . uh, phone. Maybe even drop by."

Duffy walked out of the kitchen with Joe on his shoulder.

"Well, let's see. There was a Boots . . . your aunt took the call. Bad connection, she said, but he sounded like he wanted to talk with you. She told him you'd be coming back here for supper, and to pick up Joe."

Duffy's face fell. And I sat down on the bench in our hall, my knees suddenly made of instant pudding.

"How much time do you think we've got?" I hissed at Duffy, after my dad went back to the kitchen. "A minute?"

"I don't k-know," Duffy croaked, taking Dr. Flamel's charm from his pocket. "But, can you get me a string or something so I can hang this around my neck? If it's any good, it should work better that way."

He handed me the charm and I threw it on the floor.

"Forget the charm! I'm going to get my hockey stick, and if you're smart, you'll take my spare!"

"*Bok,*" shrieked Niagara Joe and flew off Duffy's shoulder. He landed on the floor by the charm, and curious about it like he was about everything else, he picked it up and walked into the dining room.

"Hey!" Duffy yelled. "Give me that!"

Scared by Duffy's unexpected anger at him, Joe took off in one of his short, lame duck attempts to fly across the room.

"Get him," Duffy shouted, stumbling to his feet. "He's got my charm!"

I tried to hold Duffy back, but he was too upset. "Duffy, stop! You're scaring him!"

Duffy lunged again and Niagara Joe fluttered in a half circle from the corner of the stereo to a spot under the dining room buffet. Then he started walking—running, almost—for the kitchen and his Tiny Traveler.

"Niagara Joe! Come back here!"

My father stepped away from the kitchen table just as Joe came racing across the floor with Duffy's charm in his beak.

"Dad! Watch out!"

My dad froze with one foot poised above Joe's back, and Joe took off again in a frantic flight for safety. Duffy's charm skidded along the floor toward Dodger's water dish.

And Niagara Joe landed in a big bowl of stew that my father had just put down on the table.

"*Joe!*" Duffy cried and plunged his hand into the steaming hot gravy.

The doorbell rang.

"Good grief," my father gasped. "Peter, get a towel!"

Duffy turned around in tears, globs of thick brown gravy dripping off his fingers. In his hand, along with a few carrots and several peas, was a sodden Niagara Joe and his eyes were closed.

The doorbell rang again.

"I-I think he's dead," Duffy moaned and held Joe out for us to see.

Dodger was out in the hall barking.

"For heaven's sake, come in," my father shouted when the bell rang again. "Duffy, what about your hand? Peter, hold out that towel."

Shaking, I thrust the towel forward and Duffy put Joe in it. Then we rushed him to the sink where I sprayed cool water on Joe's feathers and my father applied first aid to the burns on Duffy's hand.

Dodger was still barking and I could hear someone in the hall.

"Oh, Joe, I'm sorry," Duffy cried, impatient to get his hand free from my dad, who was wrapping it. "No, it doesn't hurt much, Mr. Finley. Careful, Peter, a little more water on his wing feathers. Now around his feet, Peter . . . and his tail."

Working feverishly, I cleaned Joe off and carried his limp body to the table on a clean towel.

Duffy's burns weren't bad, but he was pale. "If I hadn't acted so stupid about that dumb charm, this never would have happened!"

That reminded me that the charm was still on the floor

somewhere, but when I glanced down, it was in splinters.

"Duffy? Dodger must have . . ."

But then, who really cared? All thoughts were on Joe.

"Is he alive?" my father asked, looking over Duffy's shoulder.

"I'm not sure," I said and touched Joe's feet lightly with the tip of my finger.

"He moved a little," Duffy croaked. "Joe? Are you still there?"

Niagara Joe pulled one of his rumpled wings closer to his body and twitched, but he did not stand up.

"Are his eyes open?" someone said in a concerned voice.

"They're just slits," I replied. "But he's not dead."

I didn't add the word "yet," because I didn't want to give up hope. And there still might be a way to save Joe. There had to be.

My dad picked up the phone. "I'm calling our doctor, Duffy's aunt and the vet, in that order. To let them know we're on our way over and find out if there's anything more we can do right now."

"Dr. Clark's good with birds," the unfamiliar voice suggested helpfully after my dad had completed the first two calls. "He took care of my grandmother's budgie once."

I turned around as my dad said, "That's fine, because

Clark's our vet, too. Hello, can I speak to the doctor, please? This is an emergency."

Standing in the doorway was a girl with a good tan and a Prince Valiant haircut. She was wearing what looked like her father's shirt, but I didn't notice much else about her. I was too busy helping Duffy.

"Is there anything I can do?" the girl asked shyly.

My father motioned to her to stay, then nodded, said yes a few more times into the receiver and hung up.

"The doctor wants to see Duffy's hand, so we're going to meet him at the hospital after we pick up Aunt Peggy. As for Joe, Dr. Clark says to smear him all over with baby oil. Or salad oil. Lucky we have some of that."

Duffy's tear-stained face was bent close over Joe's body and he was cooing softly. "You can make it, Joe. I know you can. We're going to take you to the vet. And (sniff) he's going to fix you up fine."

My dad handed me the oil and went out to start the car. "Spoon it on him as fast as you can, but don't get any in his mouth or breathing passages. I'll pull around to the driveway and wait."

The girl helped as we soaked Joe with oil.

"Who are you anyway?" I asked and Duffy glanced up.

The two of us had folded Joe's towel into a hammock-like stretcher and were on our way out the door.

"I'm Boots McAfee," the girl said, hurrying after us. "From *Help Is Here.*"

We nearly had a rear-end collision. We stopped that suddenly.

Chapter 12

"YOU'RE B-BOOTS?" Duffy choked. "But you're a girl!"

My father honked the horn and we came to life again.

"Of course, I'm a girl," she snapped. "No reason why I shouldn't be. A girl can run a business as well as a boy!" Her voice dropped to a low whisper. "But this is no time to talk about that. You'd better get to the doctor. I can deal with you later. When you come back."

"Okay," I stammered from the car window. "But I c-can't tell you when that'll be."

What was she there alone for anyway? Did she think she could fight us? Or was her gang hiding somewhere outside the house, ready for action?

There wasn't time to look, because in the next second we

were on our way and I was helping Duffy comfort Joe.

At the hospital, Captain Smiles met us in his skipper's costume. The nurses were all looking at him funny-like, but he didn't seem to care. He'd left the studio right after Aunt Peggy'd called him. And in the middle of the show, so they had to fill in with cartoons.

Duffy was astonished. "Uncle Ralph!" he said.

"Hi, kid," Captain Smiles replied shakily.

To my surprise, he was even more upset about Duffy's accident than Aunt Peggy. If that was possible. And the doctor nearly threw him out of the examination room because of it.

I thought that was unfair. It wasn't the Captain's fault that an intern made a remark about Duffy's size.

The Captain answered him with a blast so loud it brought a nurse running. "You calling my kid a pantywaist? Well, he's got more spunk than the lot of you put together and . . . brains he hasn't even used yet!"

I glanced at my father and exchanged a grin. Was Captain Smiles beginning to appreciate Duffy? It sure looked like it.

Later, we found another reason to smile—when we left the vet's with some good news about Joe.

"So he loses most of his feathers," I soothed Duffy, who

was carrying Joe in a shoebox. "They'll grow back. And good old Joe'll be sitting on his perch the same as always . . . tomorrow, when he's out of shock."

Duffy nodded, but the stricken look he'd acquired earlier never left his face.

It was still there when my dad took us all back to our place to pick up Duffy's things.

"Looks like you have company waiting for you on the front porch," Aunt Peggy observed as we turned in the driveway.

"Boots!" I gulped and scrunched down in my seat. "Duffy, it's her again," I hissed. "Can you see? Does she have her gang with her?"

I got no answer because Duffy didn't care. All that mattered to him was Joe. The rest of it just wasn't important and he lost no time in telling Boots that when we met her on the steps.

"Not important?" she gasped, as our folks disappeared into the house. "What do you mean?"

"I mean that having my own . . . business . . . just doesn't interest me anymore," Duffy croaked. "So do what you want with it. And leave me and Peter alone."

"But . . ."

"You heard him," I said, checking out the shrubs for

members of *Help Is Here*. "Wherever they are, tell your gang to lay off. We don't want a fight, and even if we did, we'd be no match for them anyway."

Boots was amazed. "You think I came here—with a gang—to make *trouble*? You have to be kidding! I just want you to be part of *Help Is Here*. As our two lawn and garden experts!"

"But your gang . . ."

"They don't know which end is up sometimes." Boots shook her head. "Honestly, muscle power is all those guys respect. They don't recognize genius when they see it. I have to show them!"

Duffy started for the door. "Well, I'm not interested," he said, trying to cradle Joe's shoebox with his bandaged hand. "Peter, if *you* want to . . ."

He was giving me a chance. "I'm not interested, either," I added flatly.

"Then be an independent organization, if you want," Boots said. "It's okay with me. But don't call it quits, Duffy. You've made too big a name for yourself."

Duffy turned and pulled himself up to his full height. "Oh, I'll be around. With Peter. Right, partner?"

"Right," I said, standing a little taller myself.

Then Duffy disappeared inside.

"But, your business . . ." Boots called after him, confused.

"Duffy doesn't need a business to feel like he's somebody," I explained. Then I grinned. "But maybe, when Joe's on the mend, he'll take it up again. You can never tell about Duffy. He's a . . . cosmic phenomenon!"

CDEFGHIJ—VB—8765432/80